THE
UNDERWORLD

a novel by

JIMMY DASAINT

This novel is a work of fiction. Any resemblance to real people, living or dead, actual events, establishments, organizations and/or locales are intended to give it a sense of reality and authenticity. Other names, characters, places and incidents are either products of the author's imagination or are used fictitiously as are those fictionalized events and incidents that involve real persons and d id not occur or are set in the future. Any character that happens to share the name of a person who is an acquaintance of the author, past or present, is purely coincidental and is in no way intended to be an actual account involving that person.

ISBN: 978-0-9823111-2-7
Author: Jimmy DaSaint
Cover Concept by Tiffany A. and LJ Graphics
Cover Design: LJ Graphics
Editing and Typesetting: Melissa Forbes, Typeset Concept by Tiffany A.

Library of Congress Cataloging-in-Publication applied for:
ISBN: 978-0-9823111-2-7
The Underworld: A novel by Jimmy DaSaint

Published by:

DaSaint Entertainment
P.O. Box 97
Bala Cynwood, PA 19004
www.DaSaintentertainment.com
dasaint@gmail.com

Printed and distributed by:

The Firm Publications
P.O. Box 2723
Philadelphia PA 19120
215-848-4385
www.TheFirmPublications.com

Copyright © 2009 by Jimmy DaSaint. All rights reserved. No part of this book may be reproduced in any form without the permission from the publisher, except by review or who may quote a brief passage to be printed in a newspaper or magazine.

Dedications

First I would like to give thanks to my Lord and savior Jesus Christ. Thanks to all the people that stood by my side while I was in my darkest moments: my mother Belinda Mathis, sisters, Dawn, Tammy, and Tanya, and my brother, Sean, my two sons, Marquise and Nigel, my ICH rap camp (SC, STONES, COLOSSUS, CHEESE, A-TOWN, YOUNG SAVAGE, BOSSMAN, SPORT, VAR, JEEKY, ELOHEMM, SHORTY RAW, T.P. DOLLAZ, SCARFO).

I want to give a special thanks to Tiona Brown (author of *Ain't No Sunshine*) for all the help and support you have given me since day one. Tiah "DC book diva," Tiff and Zahir from The Firm Publications, and all my friends in the publishing industry. Sorry, but I have too many to name.

Last but not least I can't forget all my incarcerated brothers doing time in the fed and state prisons. Keep y'all heads up and never give up on your dreams

"When two powers make war against each other, the anger and hatred that arise can be appeased only by the death of one or the other."
-J. Glenn Gary

The fire of hell is described as the rising of the
Hearts, showing that it is within the heart
Of a man that the origin of hell fire lies.
A man's hell is thus within his own heart
In his life. –The Quran
Sura 104, Verse 7

Chapter 1

Friday night

INSIDE A SMALL ROOM IN THE back of a private club, five men sat around a table talking. Another man and woman stood against the wall listening to everything that was being said. The five men at the table were Vega Littles, one of the most feared drug kingpins in the city of Philadelphia, Raymond "Butcher" Smith, Vega's right hand man and violent street enforcer, Sean "Homicide" Drayton, Vega's six-feet, seven-inch, 320-pound bodyguard, Detective Artie Fletcher, a crooked Philadelphia police officer who was on Vega's payroll, and Junie, Vega's loyal uncle.

"I think it's time that we send a message to Underworld to show him that we are serious!" Vega vented.

"I'm all in. Fuck Underworld!" Butcher yelled. "He had his run. Now it's our turn to take over this city. And what they did to Tony is something I'll never forget as long as I live. So I say let's get this shit poppin'!"

Artie stood. He looked around at everyone inside the room. Emotions were running high, and he needed to bring them all back down to reality. "I don't think it's a wise move!" Artie shouted. "Underworld is a very powerful man, not only in this city, but in every major city on the East Coast. A move like this could backfire if it's not done right. Gentlemen, we are dealing with the boss of the underworld himself. Why wake up a sleeping giant?"

"Fuck Underworld!" Butcher yelled again. "He's in our way, and unless we want to keep sharing the wealth in this city, he's gonna always be in the way!"

Vega stood from the table and looked around the room. "Junie, what do you think?" he asked.

"It's your move. I got your back no matter what."

"Homicide, what about you?"

"I say let's go. At least do it for Tony."

"And you, Butcher?"

"We should've started the war already!" he said.

"Artie?"

"I don't think we should do it yet. But whatever you do decide, I have your back 100 percent."

After a long sigh, Vega looked around at everyone and said, "With great risk comes great reward. It's time for Underworld to pass the torch, or have the torch taken from him. It's on!"

Smiles came to everyone's faces except Artie's. Deep in his heart he knew that it was the worst mistake they could ever make. Lust, greed, and money were the reasons for a lot of people's downfalls, and he was sure they would be the reasons for the downfall of Vega.

Vega looked over at the young man and woman who were standing against the wall and finally addressed them. "Junie will get y'all two of everything y'all need. And our inside source will make sure the targets are in place."

The young man and woman nodded. This was what they lived for.

As Junie walked out of the room, the man and woman followed behind him.

"Gentlemen, there can only be one king," Vega said and laughed loudly. What no one in the room knew was that Vega possessed a very deep secret. And what he was plotting to do was more personal than anything they could ever imagine.

Outside the club

Sitting inside a dark blue Ford Taurus, two FBI agents kept a close eye on the club. Special Agent Dean Mitchell had a pen and pad in his hand, writing down the license plates of all the expensive vehicles that were parked in front of the club. There was a red Lexus, a white Cadillac truck, a blue Range Rover, and a few other nice cars.

After he finished writing down his notes, he looked over at his partner, Special Agent Ronald Stokes and said, "This is some bullshit! In order for us to get close to these guys, or Frank and his underworld organization, we're gonna need a valuable inside source."

"Don't you worry," Stokes said. "We'll get one sooner or later."

Suddenly the front door of the club opened and people started walking outside. The two agents watched as the people climbed into their expensive automobiles and drove off in different directions.

"Let's get out of here," Mitchell said. "Tomorrow we're going by the prison to talk with our two informants. Maybe our luck will be better."

Miami, Florida
Saturday afternoon

Standing in front of the beautiful Ritz-Carlton Hotel, a black man holding two large black suitcases waited patiently. Finally a cab pulled up and beeped the horn. The man rushed over and got inside. After he shut the door, the cab pulled off. The cabbie didn't ask the tall black man a single question. He had already been told what to do. Plus, he had made this trip many times before. After the cabbie turned onto Collins Avenue, he drove a few blocks and then parked his cab behind a sky blue Rolls Royce Phantom. Two Latino men sat inside the Phantom—one behind the wheel, and the other—an older man—in the backseat. The black man calmly got out the cab with the two suitcases. When the Rolls Royce's trunk popped open, the man placed both suitcases inside and carefully closed the trunk. Then he walked around and got into the backseat of the car.

"My good friend, as always it's a pleasure to see you again," the older man said.

"You too, Mr. Sanchez," Frank Simms, Jr., also known as the infamous Underworld, said, shaking his hand.

Juan Sanchez was Frank's Columbian drug supplier. Juan and his Columbian cartel were responsible for 30 percent of the cocaine that entered the U.S. Outside his illegal empire, Juan Sanchez was a well-respected and powerful businessman. He was the owner of a chain of Columbian restaurants, many other residential properties, and several car dealerships. But behind his businessman image, Juan Sanchez was also one of the most powerful drug lords in the entire world.

"How is that pretty fiancée of yours doing?" Mr. Sanchez asked.

"She's fine, waiting for me at the hotel."

"So you decided to bring her with you this time?"

"Yeah, we both needed to get away for a few days. The company can be draining sometimes. A vacation was overdue."

Mr. Sanchez nodded. The man behind the wheel kept his eyes focused out the window.

"So was that everything?" Mr. Sanchez asked.

"Yes, Mr. Sanchez, every single penny."

"Very good, my friend. Your shipment will arrive in Philadelphia in a few days."

After shaking hands again, Frank opened the door to leave, but Mr. Sanchez grabbed his arm.

"Yes, Mr. Sanchez? What is it?"

"Do you like the new car I sent you for your birthday?" he asked.

"The Maybach is beautiful. Thank you."

"You're welcome, my friend."

Mr. Sanchez watched as Frank got back inside the cab. After the cab pulled off, the Rolls Royce made a U-turn and drove in the opposite direction.

South Beach

When Frank returned to his elegant suite at the Ritz-Carlton Hotel, he shut the door and rushed toward the master bedroom. Inside the room, his beautiful fiancée had her gorgeous naked body lying across the large king-sized bed. Their favorite song by the talented singer Janell Jones flowed from the bedroom speakers. A few scented candles sat on opposite sides of the bed, filling the room with a pungent, tropical, exotic smell.

Frank stared at his beautiful bride-to-be and shook his head. *What a lucky man I am,* he thought. From head to toe, Cassie was the most beautiful woman he had ever laid eyes on.

"Are you just gonna stand there and stare at me all day long, or are you gonna come join me," she asked teasingly.

Frank quickly started undressing. Once he was completely naked, he walked over and joined his fiancée in bed.

"Did anyone call me while I was gone?" he asked, rubbing his strong hands into her shoulders.

"Yeah, I spoke to your parents and Craig," she said, enjoying the wonderful pleasure of his hands.

"What did they say?" he asked as he moved his hands down her spine.

"Your mother misses you like always. She told me to take it easy on you and make sure we both say our prayers before bed."

Frank smiled and shook his head.

"Your mom is a trip," Cassie added.

"What did my father say?"

"He said to make sure you come by the church when you get back. He has something very important to tell you."

"He never said what it was?"

"No. He said that he needed to tell you face-to-face."

"Yeah, but you know how he forgets sometimes," Frank said, now rubbing his hands around her firm ass.

"You know whatever it is, he's gonna write it all down inside his daily journal." Frank smiled, knowing that she was exactly right. Whenever his father had something important on his mind, he would write it down inside his journal so he wouldn't forget.

"What did Craig say?" Frank asked.

"Nothing much. Just asked how we were doing, and said don't worry, he's back home holding down the fort. Oh, he did mention something about some interviews and photo shoots you have to do next week."

"Yeah, Riley already told me," Frank said as he turned Cassie onto her back.

"After talking to Craig, I turned off both of our cell phones. I don't want anyone else to disturb us."

"Whatever you wish, my queen," Frank said as he started kissing her soft, erect nipples.

Cassie closed her eyes and spread both arms across the bed. The man glided his tongue down to her pierced navel, sending chills throughout her body.

"Mmmm." She moaned softly.

After he spread her legs, Frank thrust his tongue into the wetness of her inviting paradise. Once again, her light moans escaped into the air, mixing with the tropical scented candles and Janell Jones's soulful voice.

Downtown Philadelphia

The federal detention center in Philadelphia was a tall brick building that housed federal inmates who were waiting to go to trial, or waiting to be transferred to their new prison destinations. Most of the prisoners inside FDC were waiting their turns to be given lengthy federal sentences, mostly for drug and gun charges.

Inside a small private room on the first floor of the building, FBI agents Mitchell and Stokes listened to the statements from their two informants. Anthony Wright and Kevin Smith were once two well-known drug dealers. Now they were FBI informants, desperately trying to get twenty-year sentences off their backs.

"Man, I'm telling you, Vega and Underworld hate each other!" Anthony said. "I know both of them! Vega wants Underworld's spot. And plus, word on the streets is that Underworld was responsible for Vega's brother's death."

"Yeah, and some people think that Underworld had Vega's parents killed in that car accident a few years ago," Kevin added.

The two agents wrote down everything on a pad while Anthony and Kevin continued to spill their guts. The agents knew that most of the stuff they were saying was all bogus info, but they wrote it down anyway.

An hour later, after the two informants were escorted back to their cells by the COs, Mitchell and Stokes walked out of the FDC and got back into their unmarked car. Unfortunately their informants hadn't given them any earth-shattering information. Their investigation was shaping up to be a long and tedious endeavor.

One of the COs who had taken the two informants back to their cells now stood outside in the back parking lot. Another CO soon walked up and stood beside him.

"You calling Craig?" the first CO asked.

"I'm about to now," the second CO said, taking out his cell phone.

After dialing a number, they both stood around waiting.

"Yo, speak," a male voice answered on the second ring.

"Yo, C, this is me, Courtney. I'm at work. I'm just calling to let you know that we found out who the informants are. The feds just left 'em."

"Well y'all know what to do. Try to make it happen before they leave that place," Craig said.

"Don't worry, C, we got you," the CO names Courtney answered.

After Courtney ended the call, he looked at his friend and said, "They can't leave FDC alive."

With a nod from the other CO, they both turned and walked back toward the building.

The contracts were now placed on the two informants' heads. And both of the COs knew that once the two jailhouse snitches were eliminated, the COs would reap the rewards for their services. No one knew that the two correctional officers were on Underworld's payroll. And they were just two of so many others.

Chapter 2

Sunday

THE AFTERNOON SUN WAS BEAMING down over the city of Philadelphia. The temperature was hovering in the high eighties. Today was the perfect day, perfect for murder. A block away from the Holy Tabernacle Baptist Church, two people on their motorcycles sat waiting patiently. Both bikers were dressed in black and carried a loaded 9 mm pistol inside their jackets.

They watched as the jubilant churchgoers exited the crowded church. Finally after twenty minutes, they spotted the two people for whom they were waiting. Quickly, they both put on their Shoei helmets and started up their bikes. Canon sat on his yellow and black Yamaha YZF-R1, and his partner in crime, Spade, rode a green and white Ducati 1098. Canon looked over at Spade and nodded. After Spade returned the nod, they sped off down the street.

Standing outside the church's front doors were Reverend Frank Simms and his wife, Clara. The couple was posing for pictures with some of their members. Standing just a few feet away was Deacon Harris, one of Reverend Simms's closest friends. Suddenly the loud roaring sounds of motorcycles interrupted the picture ceremony. When Deacon Harris turned around to see what was causing all the commotion, the two motorcycles were less than twenty feet away, with riders who were brandishing pistols.

Frank stood there completely frozen. He couldn't believe what he was seeing. His wife Clara quickly grabbed his arm in an attempt to get out of harm's way by escaping into the safety of the crowd, but it was too late.

Before either of them could run for shelter, a barrage of 9 mm bullets brought them both down. Death was instant. As the loud screams and cries erupted from the stunned crowd, the two motorcycles sped off down the street, disappearing in a matter of seconds.

Deacon Harris quickly rushed over to his friend's side. Blood was everywhere. As tears fell from his terrified eyes, he shouted, "Somebody call an ambulance! Hurry! Please, Lord, don't let him die."

A large group of stunned spectators stood around the two mangled bodies. Tears fell from every face in the shocked crowd. No one could believe their eyes.

Deacon Harris held the reverend's dead body in his trembling arms as he cried like a child. Lying right next to the reverend was his dead wife, Clara. Reverend Simms and his wife were two of the nicest people that anyone could ever know. But once the contracts were placed on their heads, it was only a matter of time before the messengers of death called their names.

Forty-five minutes later
Southwest Philadelphia

The two motorcycles pulled into an open garage and parked. Junie quickly closed the garage door behind them. Together the three walked into the house.

Inside the plush living room, Vega sat on the leather sectional with an attractive white woman lying across his lap. A short, attractive Asian woman walked into the living room and joined them.

"Ladies, give me a few minutes. I have some important business to discuss," Vega said.

Both women quickly got up and walked out of the room. Canon and Spade took off their helmets. Vega looked at his two young assassins, smiled, and shook his head. Canon was a tall, twenty-four-year-old man with a dark brown complexion and average features. And Spade was his twenty-three-year-old girlfriend. Spade was short with light skin, short, curly black hair and a set of piercing hazel eyes. Together they made one hell of a couple.

"Everything is done," Canon said.

"I know," Vega said. "My friend called and gave me the details."

"So who's next, Vega?" Spade asked.

"Calm down, pretty. My source said that the police are all over the place. We have to wait till things calm down a little before we proceed any further. In the meantime, I want y'all to lay low."

"We need a ride back home," Canon said.

"Don't worry. Junie will drive y'all back to your house, and both of the bikes will be destroyed. For now I need y'all to go upstairs and change back into your regular clothes."

Canon and Spade both turned around and walked out of the room.

"Junie, did you call Butcher and Artie?" Vega asked.

"Yeah, boss. They're gonna meet you at the club tonight at eight thirty," Junie answered.

"Good. I need to discuss our next move," Vega said as he stood. Dressed in a long, black silk robe and matching slippers, Vega walked over to the steps. "Where are the girls?" he asked.

"Upstairs waiting in the master bedroom, boss."

"OK, good. I don't want to be disturbed for a few hours. After you drop off Canon and Spade, make sure you check on things before you come back here."

"No problem, boss."

Vega walked up the stairs and down the long hall. When he entered the large master bedroom, the two beautiful women were locked in a passionate kiss.

"Ladies, y'all couldn't wait for me?" Vega asked, dropping the robe to the floor and revealing his muscular, naked body. Although Vega stood at just five feet nine inches tall, he was built like an NFL linebacker. He had dark, caramel skin and kept his head shaved completely bald. "Ain't no fun if daddy can't have none," he said, walking over and joining the two women in bed.

Vega was a thirty-three-year-old man who enjoyed the finer things in life—beautiful, exotic women, European cars, and expensive jewelry. His crew was bringing him in over a million dollars each month. He had crooked cops and young assassins on his team that made sure everything ran smoothly. But today was like no other day before. Vega had made one of his most important moves by having his number one enemy's parents brutally murdered outside their church.

The murders were meant to send out a powerful message, but Vega's decision to kill Underworld's parents was more personal than anyone knew.

After changing out of their black motorcycle outfits and back into their regular clothes, Canon and Spade walked into the living room where Junie was waiting.

"Y'all ready?" he asked.

"Yeah. We left the guns in the room with the other clothes," Canon said as he and Spade followed Junie over to the front door.

"Good. I'll destroy everything together," Junie said, opening the door.

After they walked outside, they all climbed into a dark blue Range Rover.

"Where to?" Junie asked as he started up the Range.

"You can drop us off on South Street," Spade said.

Junie turned up the radio and pulled off down the quiet, deserted street.

Spade laid her head across Canon's lap. She was the true love of his life. And he was hers. Since meeting five years earlier, they had been inseparable. When you saw one, the other was never too far away. For two years they had been working with Vega as hired assassins. He paid well, and in return they did the jobs that no one else had the guts to do.

Junie parked the Range Rover on the corner of Twelfth and South streets. After Canon and Spade got out of the SUV and shut the doors, Junie rolled down the tinted window and said, "I'll call y'all in a few days. Have fun."

Then he rolled up the window and quickly drove off. Spade reached out and grabbed Canon's hand. Together they walked down the crowded street, both smiling from ear to ear. No one would ever imagine that the two young lovebirds were ruthless killers who had just murdered an elderly preacher and his wife in cold blood.

Chapter 3

South Beach

INSIDE THE SPACIOUS LALOCANDA ITALIAN restaurant, Frank and his beautiful fiancée, Cassie, were seated at a private table in the back. For three days they had been enjoying the lovely city of Miami. Their private suite inside the Ritz-Carlton gave them a wonderful view of the city.

Frank looked across the table at his beautiful fiancée and smiled. For five years she had been the love of his life. Cassie reached out her hands and grabbed his.

"Thanks for bringing me with you this time," she said.

"Anything for you, beautiful," Frank replied, gently squeezing her hands. For a few moments they just stared into each other's eyes, lost in their own fantasies.

Frank "Underworld" Simms Jr. was a thirty-four-year-old handsome man. He stood six feet even with caramel-brown skin, short, wavy hair, and light brown eyes. Frank was the CEO and founder of Underworld Entertainment, an entertainment company that promoted large concerts and signed up and coming musicians, rappers, actors, and singers. He also produced, directed, and distributed urban films on the East Coast that went straight to DVD. Besides owning one of the most successful entertainment companies in the U.S., Frank was also one of the most powerful men in the illegal world of drugs.

On the streets of Philly, New York, DC, Baltimore, Camden, and parts of Delaware and Virginia, Frank Simms Jr. was known by one name only—Underworld, the boss of the Underworld drug cartel.

"Are you upset with me for making you leave your cell phone in the hotel room?" Cassie asked.

"Not at all. I'm sure Craig is making sure that everything back in Philly is right. Today it's all about us," Frank said, staring across the table.

"Are you ready to take this back to our cozy hotel suite? I'm really looking forward to another lovemaking session inside the Jacuzzi," Cassie said.

"Then what are we waiting for?" Frank asked as they both stood from the table.

After paying the bill with his platinum Visa, Frank and Cassie walked out of the restaurant and got inside the waiting limousine. The driver quickly pulled away, headed back to the Ritz-Carlton. Inside the privacy of the limo, Frank and Cassie embraced in a long, passionate kiss.

Philadelphia

Craig was seated at his desk with his head hanging low. A stream of tears fell from his eyes. He reached for his cell and once again dialed Frank's number. But the voicemail picked up again. Frustrated, he slammed down his cell phone. He had been trying to reach Frank for over an hour.

Craig picked up his cell phone again and called someone else.

"Yo, Craig, what's up?" a man's voice asked, picking up on the second ring.

"Graveyard, something terrible has happened. I'm gonna need you to catch a flight to Philly as soon as possible. This is an emergency," Craig said.

"Where is Underworld?" Graveyard asked.

"He's in Miami. Look, I can't say that much right now. Just catch a plane and get here!"

"I'm on my way," Graveyard said, closing his cell phone.

After hanging up with Graveyard, Craig tried to get in contact with Frank one more time. But once again the voicemail picked up.

"Frank, this is Craig. Please call me back as soon as possible. We have a major problem!"

Craig closed his cell phone, stood, and walked over to the window. He still couldn't believe that someone had put a hit out on Frank's parents. And now they were both dead. Deep in his heart Craig knew that Vega was the man responsible. Underworld and Vega hated each other with a passion. But this act of violence was the furthest that any of them had ever gone to show their hatred.

Craig Morris was Frank's best friend and right hand man, as well as the vice president of Underworld Entertainment. They had been best friends since the fifth grade. Craig was a tall, brown-skinned man with handsome features. He had degrees in accounting and finance from Drexel University. He was also the man responsible for most of the major moves that Frank made. Frank trusted Craig with his life, and Craig felt the same way.

Staring out the window, Craig still couldn't believe that Mr. and Mrs. Simms had been brutally gunned down. As the tears continued to fall, all Craig could do was shake his head in total disbelief.

Cleveland, Ohio

On the corner of 169th Street and Glendale Avenue, Graveyard watched for his cab to arrive. Graveyard was a slim, dark-skinned man who stood around five feet ten inches tall. His body was filled with tattoos to cover the scars from a lifetime of violence.

After waiting for thirty minutes, the yellow cab finally pulled to the curb and stopped. Graveyard quickly got inside the cab and closed the door.

"Where to, buddy?" the cabbie asked.

"Airport," Graveyard said.

Graveyard thought about the phone call he'd gotten from Craig and wondered what was. wrong. He knew that whatever it was, it had to be major. The last time Craig had called him with such urgency, he was paid to execute a drug dealer named Tony Littles. A few days later, Tony's body was found floating in the Schuylkill River without his head attached. The head was discovered later on a baseball field in Camden, New Jersey.

Graveyard and Frank met a few years earlier in Las Vegas. Both men were there for business. They instantly hit it off, and soon Frank was flying Graveyard out to Philly on a regular basis. Graveyard would take care of Frank's business, get paid, and catch a plane back to Cleveland. It was all very organized and neat, and the physical distance between Frank and Graveyard made it almost impossible for anyone to find Graveyard and associate him with Frank.

When the cab pulled up in front of the airport's main entrance, Graveyard paid the cabbie and got out. With fake ID in hand, he rushed toward the American Airlines terminal.

Miami

Inside the comfort of their lavish private suite, Frank lay in the warm Jacuzzi watching Cassie get undressed. Cassie Lopez was a tall, beautiful half-black and half-Puerto Rican woman with the looks of a supermodel. She had a dark brown complexion and a body with curves in all the right places. Her long, black, silky hair hung down to the center of her back. At thirty, Cassie looked as if she was ten years younger.

After unsnapping her bra and tossing it to the floor, Cassie smiled, then slid down her red thong and stepped out of it. She walked over to the bubbling warm Jacuzzi and joined her handsome fiancé. Their naked bodies instantly became one as the two started passionately kissing. Cassie climbed on top of Frank's rock hard manhood and wrapped her arms around his neck. She slowly rode him into a world of pure ecstasy.

Just a few feet away, Frank's cell phone continued to vibrate. Neither of the lovers paid it any mind.

CHAPTER 4

Later that night

THE DOLLHOUSE GENTLEMEN'S CLUB WAS located in a secluded area in Center City, Philadelphia. Vega had purchased the property a year earlier from its original owner. The place was large and spacious with a long wooden stage and small tables situated throughout. Homicide, who acted as the security guard for the club, stood at the front entrance, watching as the white Cadillac truck pulled up and parked. He quickly ran over and opened the door. Vega stepped out wearing a gold silk outfit and matching alligator sandals. Junie got out of the truck and followed Vega and Homicide inside the club.

Once inside they all walked straight to the back. When they entered two men were sitting at a round table talking. There was a large black briefcase lying on top of the table. Homicide pulled out a chair for Vega. After Vega was seated, Homicide walked away, and Junie found himself an empty chair and sat down.

"What's up, boss?" Artie asked, noticing the serious look on Vega's face.

"What did y'all find out this afternoon?" Vega asked.

"I was called down to the scene with a few other officers, and so far there are no clues. All the witnesses had to say was that they saw two men on motorcycles drive up and start shooting at the reverend and his wife.

There was a lot of confusion. From all my years on the police force, I would call it a perfect double homicide," Artie replied with a grin.

"Good. Keep me posted on anything new that comes up."

"You got it, boss," Artie said.

"Where's Canon and Spade?" Butcher asked.

"Who knows where those two are. I told 'em that I would call 'em in a few days," Vega said. "Butcher, how's my drug business coming along?"

"Everything is wonderful, boss. We should be ready for another shipment very soon," Butcher said, pushing the briefcase toward Vega.

"How much is this?"

"Six hundred thousand. I'll have the rest by Wednesday."

"Is everybody ready for what's soon to come?" Vega asked.

"We have no choice but to be ready," Butcher said. "Underworld will come after us with everything he's got."

"An eye for an eye," Vega said. "That was revenge for my brother Tony. May his soul rest in peace."

"I still think we should've waited a while," Artie said.

"And why's that, Artie?" Vega asked.

"Because Underworld is a very powerful man who is connected with other powerful people. I still think it was a bad idea to kill his parents. This only adds fuel to the fire. We should've waited for the perfect opportunity. Sooner or later Underworld would've slipped up."

"Fuck Underworld and his parents!" Vega shouted. "They deserved it! He started this war when he had my brother murdered! I'm tired of playing this game of cat and mouse. And I'm even more tired of sharing the city's drug profits. I want it all! Every dollar that's made off drugs in this city, I want ninety-five cents. And the only way for me to get that is by killing my enemy and everything he loves."

"All I'm saying is we could've gone about it in another way."

"I did what I did, and now it's done! The hell with 'em. They were two evil old bastards anyway!"

"Artie, you just do what we pay you for, and let us gangsters worry about the streets," Butcher added.

"Yeah, can you do that, Officer Artie Fletcher?" Vega asked sarcastically.

"As long as y'all keep paying me, I'll do whatever," Artie responded.

Vega opened the briefcase and stared at all the neat stacks of money. There was ten thousand dollars in each stack. He reached inside, grabbed two stacks, and tossed both stacks to Artie.

"Keep your ear to the streets. That's what I pay you for. And from now on keep all your personal feelings to yourself," Vega said.

Artie placed both stacks inside his jacket. Then he stood and walked over to Vega.

"You got it, boss. Tell your wife I said hi. And don't worry, I'll keep you posted on anything new." After shaking everyone's hands, Artie walked out of the room and exited the club through a back door.

"So what do you think, boss?" Butcher asked.

"Artie will be all right. As long as he gets paid, he don't care who lives or dies," Vega said, standing up and closing the briefcase. Vega took the briefcase and all three men exited the room. When they walked to the front entrance, Homicide was standing outside the door.

"Homicide, I will see you tomorrow night." Vega said.

"OK, boss," Homicide said in a deep baritone voice.

"Butcher, I'll call you in the morning."

"All right, boss. Tell Raquel I said hi. Bye, Junie," Butcher said as he walked toward his brand new red Lexus coupe.

"Take care, Butcher," Junie said as he and Vega climbed back inside the Cadillac truck.

After Junie started up the truck, Vega looked over and said, "So what do you think of the decision I made?"

"Only time will tell, boss." Junie said as he stared straight into Vega's eyes. Then he put the truck in drive and pulled off down the dark street.

Before Vega could ask another question, his cell phone rang. He looked at the caller ID and quickly answered.

"Hello, my love. I'm on my way home now."

"Baby, can you bring me a pint of chocolate ice cream?" his wife Raquel asked.

"Your wish is my command," Vega said with a smile.

Downtown Philly

The young female prostitutes always came out late at night. And the johns who enjoyed paying for sex were never far away. FBI agents Mitchell and Stokes sat in their vehicle across from Underworld Entertainment as the prostitutes paraded down the dimly lit street. Whenever the agents were on their late night stakeouts, they always preferred to park the car in this spot. From there they could catch the young ladies of the night while watching the front door that led to the Underworld Entertainment offices.

"Do you think Vega's got enough balls to have Frank's parents killed?" Mitchell asked.

"That's like committing suicide!" Stokes responded.

"Who knows. It could've been anybody in this ruthless town. One thing for sure is they better not let Frank find out. The man practically owns this city."

"Well that won't last for long. We're on the case now. And I don't plan on letting up on Frank or Vega until they're both in federal prison. These street punks have been destroying this city for years with all their drugs and gun violence. I personally have had enough!" Stokes said.

"Calm down, partner," Mitchell said. "Everything will be all right. Tomorrow morning we have that meeting with one of the city's top assistant DAs. Maybe we'll learn some new things about Vega and Frank that will help us with our federal investigation."

"Yeah, maybe you're right," the agent said as he watched one of the young black prostitutes run over to a john's car and get inside.

New York City

Janell Jones sat on the sofa inside her private suite, thinking about her secret lover who lived two hours away in Philadelphia. She had left three messages on his voicemail, but he hadn't returned her calls.

After hearing about the tragic murders that had taken place in Philly, Janell knew she had to see him soon. A hard knock on the door startled her. She stood and walked over to the door. After looking out the small peep hole, she opened the door. Standing right there was her manager, Joe Fisher, the man who had played a major part in blowing up her singing career.

"What is it, Joe?"

"I just got off the phone with the people over at *Essence*. They'll be here on Tuesday morning."

"OK, fine. I'll make sure I'm ready. Do I have anything on the schedule for tomorrow night?"

"The Baby Phat celebrity party that you were invited to."

"Cancel it. I have something very important to do," Janell said.

Joe gave her a suspicious look. "I hope it's not what I think! Please tell me that your not gonna sneak off again and go see that thug in Philadelphia. I told you so many times that if the media was ever to find out about y'all two, it would end your singing career."

"No, that's not it," she lied. "It's late, Joe. Goodnight. I'll see you in the morning," Janell said, closing the door in his face.

Miami

Inside their lavish presidential suite, only the sounds of intense lovemaking could be heard. Frank and Cassie were on top of the large king-sized bed, making love like they were the last two people alive. Sweat covered both of their naked bodies.

A hard knock at the door interrupted their sexual interlude. Frank got up and grabbed his silk robe from the floor. After putting it on, he walked out of the bedroom. Cassie lay in bed, holding on to one of the thick pillows, trying to calm her breathing.

When Frank opened the door, a short man in a green jacket and tan slacks stood there.

"Sorry to disturb you, sir. My name is Vincent. I'm the hotel manager. We've been trying to call you, but apparently your room phone is off the hook."

"Yeah, we didn't want to be disturbed," Frank said. "What's the problem?"

"A young man by the name of Craig has been calling you from Philadelphia. He said that it's very important that you call him. He's been trying to reach you on your cell phone as well. He sounded very concerned about something. I'm sorry to disturb you, sir, but I felt that it was very important that I relay his message," the man said.

"Thank you. I really appreciate that," Frank said, watching as the man turned and walked away. Frank shut the door and quickly ran over to his cell phone. When he checked the voicemail count, he saw that Craig had left over twenty messages.

What the hell is going on? he wondered.

Frank nervously called Craig and waited. On the second ring Craig answered.

"Frank! Frank! Frank! They killed 'em! They killed 'em, man! They killed 'em!" Craig cried out.

"Craig, calm down! Now tell me what's going on and who was killed."

"Frank, your parents, man! Your parents were killed today right outside their church! It's all over the news, man! I've been trying to call you all day long!" Craig tearfully shouted.

"No! Please, God, don't let this be true! Nooooo!" Frank screamed.

Cassie quickly jumped up from the bed and grabbed her silk robe. When she ran into the living room, Frank was on his knees in tears.

"Frank, what is it?" Cassie asked with a worried look on her face.

"They killed my parents!" Frank yelled.

Cassie fell to her knees by his side and wrapped her arms around him.

"No! No! Why, God. Why!" Frank cried out in anguish.

Craig continued to hold on the phone, but he didn't say another word. He could hear Frank and Cassie both crying in the background. Craig knew that Vega had crossed the ultimate line. And Frank would not rest until Vega and everything he loved in life was dead and gone.

Chapter 5

West Philadelphia
Forty-third Street and Westminster Avenue

INSIDE THEIR SMALL ROW HOUSE, Canon and Spade sat on the couch cleaning their collection of guns. Two .40 calibers, a 10 mm, silencers, and boxes of ammunition were all lying on the coffee table. The large flat screen TV was tuned to the local news. Spade quickly picked up the remote control and turned up the volume up.

"This is reporter Chuck Reynolds of the CBS Evening News. This afternoon a terrible incident occurred. The popular Baptist minister Frank Simms and his wife of thirty-four years, Clara Simms, were both savagely gunned down right outside the Holy Tabernacle Baptist Church. Witnesses have told us that two gunmen on motorcycles drove up on a crowd outside the church and started shooting at the reverend and his wife. No one else at the scene was shot or injured. The Simmses were a very popular couple around this West Philly neighborhood. They were involved with numerous events and charities to better the community. No one knows why anyone would've wanted to harm the reverend and his wife.

"Their only child is the successful businessman, Frank Simms Jr., the CEO of Underworld Entertainment. We have tried several times to reach him for comments, but so far we've been unable to contact him. Philadelphia police are looking for any clues or information that can help them with this brutal double slaying. So far they have no clues or suspects. If you have any information that can help, please call your local police station. All calls will be confidential. I'm Chuck Reynolds reporting live for the CBS Evening News."

Spade turned off the TV and looked over at Canon. Suddenly big smiles appeared on both of their faces.

"That's two more we can add to the list," Spade said.

Canon picked up a yellow pad and black pen. Eleven names were written on the pad. Spade watched Cannon added the names of Frank and Clara Simms.

"That's thirteen," Canon said excitingly.

With smiles on both their faces, they stared at each other, and began to get aroused. When they both got undressed, Spade laid her naked body across the couch. Canon slowly climbed on top of her and they started passionately kissing.

Canon and Spade had a very strange love that no one understood. They were obsessed with two things—making love and murder. In the comfort of their home, the two young assassins were now lost inside their own sexual maze. They lived in a world where there were no worries. To them, death was a beautiful thing. They felt no remorse for any of their victims, only relief and satisfaction.

City Line Avenue

Junie pulled up and parked the truck in front of a beautiful two-story home.

"Junie, when you get back to the house, tell Cindy and Jewell that I need them to do something for me in the morning," Vega said.

"OK, boss," Junie said.

"I have to make sure our friend gets the rest of his money. He did us a big favor." Vega smiled devilishly.

"A very big favor," Junie said and nodded.

"Hey, what are friends for?" Vega laughed as he opened the door and stepped out of the truck. "That's why I trust no one but you, of course," Vega said, walking toward the front door.

When Vega reached the front door, Junie slowly pulled off down the dark, quiet street. Junie was overprotective of Vega, and for that reason he was one of only a handful of people who Vega could trust.

Ever since Junie had been released from federal prison, Vega had taken him under his wing, making sure Junie would never want for anything. He gave Junie a place to live, cars to drive, and kept money in his pocket. And even though Junie didn't always agree with some of the things that Vega did, he was very loyal to his young nephew.

When Vega walked into the house, his beautiful, pregnant wife, Raquel, was sitting on the sofa patiently waiting for him. Raquel was four months pregnant with their second child. Their six-year-old daughter, Erika, was asleep upstairs in her bedroom. Vega walked over to his smiling wife and passed her a small brown bag with the pint of chocolate ice cream inside. Then he sat down beside her. Mary J. Blige's soulful melodic voice flowed from the speakers. Raquel was a big fan of the R&B diva.

"So how was your day?" she asked, cuddling up beside him.

"Beautiful. I got a lot accomplished today," Vega said with a smile.

"I saw the news earlier. That was awful what happened to Frank's parents,"

"Shit happens!" Vega replied.

"I hope you didn't have anything to do with that, Vega."

"I didn't," he lied.

"I know that y'all two can't stand each other, but killing someone's parents is going way overboard."

"I told you that I had nothing to do with it. Frank has a lot of enemies besides me. You know how this game goes, Raquel. Once you reach the top, everybody starts aiming for your head."

Raquel didn't respond. She knew that Vega wasn't telling her everything. He never did.

"You know that I love you, baby. I just want you to be safe out on those streets," Raquel said in a sincere voice.

"I told you that I'll be fine, so don't worry your pretty little self. I got this," Vega said leaning over and kissing Raquel on the lips. They both stood and walked over to the stairs. As Mary's soulful voice continued to flow out of the speakers, they walked up the steps, headed for the master bedroom.

Monday
Philadelphia International Airport

When Frank and Cassie walked out of the crowded airport's main gate, a tinted black Mercedes Benz limousine was parked outside waiting for them. The door quickly swung open and they both got inside. Seated inside the limo were Craig and Graveyard. As soon as Frank shut the door, the limo slowly pulled off. Craig reached out and gave his best friend a hug.

"I'm sorry, Frank. I'm so sorry," he said, trying his hardest to hold back the tears.

Graveyard sat back in total silence. Like always, a serious expression was plastered on his face. Graveyard was a man who rarely showed any emotions. In his line of work, showing any kind of emotion was considered a major weakness, so he kept how he felt to himself.

Cassie wrapped her arms around Frank and laid her head on his shoulder. The two of them had cried all night long.

"Craig, I want you to call a meeting for tonight. Tell everybody to be at the company at nine o'clock sharp."

"I'll get right on that."

The limousine slowed down and stopped at the corner of Eighty-fourth Street and Lindbergh Boulevard. It pulled over and parked behind a dark gray, S-600 Mercedes Benz. Frank kissed Cassie softly on the lips and said, "The limo is gonna take you straight home. Do what I told you, and I'll call you later."

"All right, baby. I'll take care of everything. I love you."

"I love you too," Frank said as he, Craig, and Graveyard all exited the limo.

They stood there watching the limo pull off down the street.

After the limo was a few blocks away, they all climbed inside Craig's Mercedes.

Graveyard did the driving while Frank and Craig sat in the backseat talking and discussing strategies.

For half an hour Graveyard just listened and occasionally nodded. Craig got on his cell phone and started calling all their top street lieutenants and major associates while Frank was on his cell phone handling other important business. Together they were formulating their master plan, making sure that all the key people were in place. Frank was connected with powerful people of wealth and political status. And most of them owed him big favors.

Graveyard pulled up and parked the car in front of Philadelphia's medical examiner's office. Frank had to be there to identify the bodies of his slain parents. Frank nervously stepped out of the car and walked over to the front entrance. When he entered the building, a strange feeling swept through his body. The reality had finally hit him like a bolt of lighting. His parents were now gone forever. And not all the money in this cruel world could bring them back. As the tears fell from his eyes, all Frank could think about was one thing—the ultimate revenge.

Chapter 6

BUTCHER WAS A THIRTY-ONE-YEAR-OLD EX-CON with a short temper and a violent attitude. He was slim, dark skinned and stood six feet even. As Vega's number one street enforcer, and the general to their illegal drug organization, Butcher was the man responsible for delivering large quantities of cocaine and heroin throughout West Philly. Vega supplied it, and Butcher delivered it.

On the streets Butcher had a reputation as a ruthless killer, a man that was well respected by few, and feared by many. Vega gave Butcher his nickname when they robbed a major drug dealer from South Philadelphia nine years earlier. After Vega had tied and duct taped the man to a wooden chair, Butcher pulled out two twelve-inch blades and started cutting up the man limb by limb. Ever since that cold winter day, Raymond Smith was known simply as Butcher.

On this day Butcher had some business to take care of. He parked his red Lexus coupe in front of a small West Philly row house where two teenage boys sat on the steps. The front door opened and a young man walked out carrying a black backpack in his hand. Butcher rolled down the window and the man tossed the back pack onto the empty passenger seat.

"How much is it, Pervis?" Butcher asked.

"Sixty grand," Pervis said.

"Good work. I'll see you tomorrow," Butcher said as he rolled up the window and pulled off down the street.

Butcher took out his cell phone and dialed a number. A man's voice answered on the second ring.

"Hello?"

"Yo, Homicide, it's me, Butcher."

"What's up?"

"Make sure the club is open on time tonight. Me and the boss will be coming through there later."

"Don't worry, Butcher. I told all the girls to be here an hour early. The workers will have everything in order."

"How's that other thing coming along?" Butcher asked as he stopped his car at a red light.

"I'ma need a few more. The white boys are buying them up. The five you gave me I already sold."

Unknown to Vega, Butcher and Homicide were selling kilos of cocaine out of the club. They were making a hundred thousand dollars each week.

When the light turned green, Butcher stepped on the gas and continued to drive down the street.

"Remember, this stays between me and you," Butcher said. "The boss thinks he's running a legitimate business, so let's just keep it that way."

"The club is a legitimate business. It's just most of our customers are crooks," Homicide said, then laughed. "Those white boys from downtown come here to turn their fantasies into realities. Where else can they get high and buy all the black pussy in the world without any worries?"

"I'll see you later, Homicide," Butcher said, ignoring Homicide's comment. "I have a few more stops to make. I'm out."

Standing outside the Holy Tabernacle Baptist Church, Deacon Harris watched as the blue Range Rover pulled up and parked. Inside the Range were two attractive women—one white and the other Asian. Deacon Harris rushed over to the SUV and got inside. The truck quickly pulled off down the street. After circling the block, Deacon Harris got out of the Range Rover holding a brown bag in his hand. Before he walked back into the church, the Range Rover was already halfway down the street.

Chestnut Hill, Philadelphia

The limousine pulled up and parked outside the two-story house. Cassie grabbed her brown leather traveling bag and quickly got out. The entire ride home she had been making lots of important calls for Frank. When Cassie entered their large, beautiful home, she kicked off her Prada shoes, threw her bag on the leather sectional, and ran over to her computer. Besides being Frank's beautiful fiancée, Cassie was the president of operations at Underworld Entertainment. She was the person who dealt with the celebrities, publicists, TV executives, and overall promotions. Cassie had a degree in business management from Howard University in Washington DC. Not only did she possess the beauty of a model, but she also had the brains to complement her beauty.

As Cassie sat in front of the computer typing, tears began falling from her eyes. She couldn't help but think about the Simmses being murdered right outside their church. From the first moment she had met them, the Simmses had welcomed Cassie into their family with loving arms. And now they were no longer here.

"Who could be so cruel?" Cassie asked aloud.

As much as Cassie had begged Frank to leave the street life alone, Cassie knew that the death of his parents would now prevent that from happening. She loved Frank more that life itself. But once Frank had made up his mind about something, there was nothing that anyone could do to change it. As tears continued to fall down her face, Cassie sat at her computer typing away.

Southwest Philly

The two beautiful women walked back into the house and shut the door. Junie and Vega were sitting on the sofa talking. Both women walked up to Vega and kissed him softly on his cheeks. Jewell was a tall, attractive white woman with light blue eyes and long blond hair. And her friend Cindy was a short Asian woman with a gorgeous face and a body to match. They were Vega's sexy mistresses, and they did whatever he told them to do.

"Did y'all take care of that?" Vega asked.

"Yes, daddy, everything is taken care of," Jewell answered.

"OK, good. Y'all can go upstairs and wait for me," Vega said as the two women turned and walked away.

After both women left the room, Vega looked over at Junie and asked, "Do you think he will keep his mouth closed?"

"I don't see why not. He has just as much to lose as us. Besides, he's now gotten the position that he's always wanted," Junie said.

"Still, I don't trust him. I'll let 'im enjoy the money for a week or so, then I want you to get in contact with Canon and Spade."

Junie calmly shook his head and said, "No problem, boss."

Craig's Mercedes Benz pulled up and parked a few blocks away from City Hall. A short white man in a blue business suit quickly got inside. The man noticed that Graveyard was the only person inside. Graveyard quickly pulled off down the crowded street. After driving a few blocks down Broad Street, Graveyard found an empty parking space behind a brand new, all black Maybach. The Maybach was tinted so no one could see inside. The white man got out of the Mercedes and calmly walked over to the Maybach and got inside.

"Pete, as always it's good to see you," Frank said as he sat comfortably in the backseat.

Craig was seated behind the steering wheel.

"Frank, I'm sorry about your parents. I—"

"What do you got for me?" Frank asked, cutting him off.

After a long sigh Pete looked at both men and said, "Some more bad news."

"What now?" Craig asked.

"The FBI is in the beginning stages of a secret investigation on you, Frank, and your entire Underworld organization. They have a few jailhouse informants working for them. They are also investigating Vega and Butcher. So far they don't have anything solid on any of y'all. I personally talked with the two FBI agents that are on the case. They were at my office early this morning."

"What did they want to know?" Frank asked curiously.

"They were just asking me a lot of questions about you. I told 'em that you're a respectable business man."

"Why would they be asking about me?"

"People are bringing up your name a lot, enough to make the feds very curious about you. You know how the game is played, Frank. The crabs at the bottom are all scheming and plotting to reach the top. With all the informants the feds have, I'm sure they know who's the real king of the underworld. And I'm not talking about your entertainment company," Pete said in a serious tone.

"Any video surveillance or wiretaps?" Frank asked.

"No. They haven't gotten that far yet. Everything is still in the beginning stages as far as I know. Your parents getting murdered didn't help matters. Sooner or later the feds are gonna put two and two together."

"Thanks, Pete. I'll call you later. Or call me when you find out more," Frank said, shaking his hand.

"Frank, just be careful, my friend. And whatever you do, do it fast and flawless," Pete said as he got out of the car.

Craig and Frank watched Pete get back inside the Mercedes. When Graveyard pulled off, Frank looked at Craig and asked, "So what do you think?"

"Well, Pete's the assistant district attorncy. If anyone knows what's going on, it's him. I talked to our men down at the prison. They found two more informants. Soon they'll be out of the way like all the others. We don't need the feds snooping around anymore than they have to. Everybody is gonna meet us later tonight. Once you run down everything to them we'll be straight. And as long as you and I continue to play the background, everything should go according to plan."

After a long sigh Frank said, "That motherfucker is gonna pay! Him and everybody he loves. Vega may have won the battle, but he will lose this war!"

Craig saw the serious expression on Frank's face and turned around. He started up the Maybach and drove down the street. When he looked through the rearview mirror he saw that Frank was lost in deep thought. He had just let the morgue after seeing his parents' shot up bodies. Craig could only imagine what was going through Frank's mind as he stared into the air, lost somewhere in a world of his very own.

Chapter 7

For three hours Graveyard drove around Philadelphia checking out things in a tinted, black Dodge Magnum. The Mercedes brought too much attention, something that Graveyard didn't like.

In a secret compartment under the seat, there were three brand new guns—a 9 mm with attached silencer, a .40 caliber, and a chrome 10 mm pistol—and a pair of night vision binoculars.

Graveyard had been driving throughout West and North Philadelphia, making sure he passed through all the major streets and avenues. With his cell phone lying between his legs, Graveyard made a turn down Market Street and headed toward South Philly.

West Philly

"Oh, yes, daddy! Yes! Oh!" Jewell yelled out as Vega pulled on her long blond hair while he fucked her hard from behind.

Vega had Jewell bent over the bed and was fucking her brains out while Cindy lay just a few feet away enjoying the live X-rated show. Vega's and Jewell's naked bodies were both covered in sweat. For the last hour Vega had been having sex with both women. Not a day went by that the three of them didn't indulge in their explicit threesomes. The girls were open to any and everything, and so was Vega.

After Jewell came for the second straight time, her tired body slumped down on the bed. Vega glanced over at Cindy with a look of sexual hunger in his eyes. Without any hesitation, Cindy crawled over toward him.

"Put your legs behind you head," he ordered.

Cindy lay back on the large king-sized bed and did as she was told. In one smooth motion Vega slid his well-endowed manhood inside Cindy's pussy, going deep as he could. Her hard, intense moans instantly filled the air. And even though there was more pain than pleasure, this was the way Cindy preferred sex—the rougher, the better.

Rolling over on the bed, Jewell lay back watching her girlfriend receive the fucking of her life.

Downstairs in the living room Junie could hear it all. It was something that he had gotten used to. Junie walked over and sat down on the sofa with a rolled up blunt inside his hand. After lighting the blunt, Junie got himself a little more relaxed on the sofa. While Vega was upstairs enjoying himself, Junie was downstairs doing the same.

Holy Tabernacle Baptist Church

"It was horrible, Frank, just horrible, and I couldn't do nothing to save them!" Deacon Harris cried out. "Nothing!"

Frank looked at the old man and sadly shook his head. Frank had known the deacon for a few years, ever since he had joined his father's church.

Deacon Harris watched as Frank paced. He could tell that Frank was deeply hurt.

"So you said it happened too fast for anyone to get a good look at the two people on the bikes?" Frank asked as he finally stopped pacing.

"Yes, Frank, there was a lot of chaos. People were running to get out of the way. I'm sorry that I can't be of more assistance, but I'm still dealing with the loss as well. I watched your father die in my arms," Deacon Harris said as a stream of tears started falling down his cheeks. "I talked to the authorities, and I told 'em all the same thing."

"Damn!" Frank yelled as he slammed his fist hard against the wall. "Have you seen any new faces attending church services lately?"

"No, Frank. None that I can recall."

Once again Frank started pacing. His heart filled with anger and revenge.

"Your parents' funeral and burial will take place this Friday. I've been getting everything prepared," the deacon said.

"So do you know who'll be the person that'll take my father's place?"

"For the time being it will be me. The congregation will have a meeting in a few weeks, and we'll decide then who it will be that will take your father's place permanently."

After a long sigh, Frank walked up to the deacon and shook his hand. "I'll see you in a few days, deacon. You take care," Frank said and sadly walked away.

"Frank."

Frank stopped and turned around. "Yes, deacon? What is it?"

"You be safe out there. I'm sure whoever did this to your parents was sending a message to you."

Frank stared into Deacon Harris's worried eyes and nodded. Then without saying another word, he turned and walked away.

After Frank climbed into the backseat of his Maybach, Craig slowly pulled off down the street.

"What did the deacon say?" Craig asked.

"Everything we already knew, but today there was something very strange about him."

"Maybe he's afraid for his life also," Craig said as he drove down Forty-sixth Street.

"I don't know what it is, but the vibe just didn't feel right."

"Where to next?" Craig asked, changing the subject.

"Back downtown. We have to go meet with Robert at his law office. Then afterward we'll go by the company and just wait for everyone to arrive," Frank said as he reached for his cell phone.

On the corner of Fifty-third and Chestnut streets, Artie sat behind the wheel of his unmarked police car. Artie had been a detective on the Philadelphia police force for seven years, and on Vega's payroll for the last two. Artie was one of Vega's most powerful weapons. He was also the man behind a lot of the violent murders and kidnappings in the city, mostly killing off rival drug dealers that gave Vega's crew competition on the streets. The only person that was out of Artie's league was Frank "Underworld" Simms, and that was what bothered him the most.

On the Philly streets Frank was untouchable, the real boss among bosses. And Artie knew this. He also knew that Frank was a man who should never be crossed, because once a person crossed that bridge, there was no turning back. Artie knew that Vega and whoever else was down with him were now all wanted men. Most people on the streets knew that Artie was one of Vega's men, and sooner or later the word would get back to Underworld.

Artie feared for his life. He knew that the only way to save himself from sure death was to find and kill the one man that scared him more than anything in this world—Frank "Underworld" Simms. After a call came in on his police radio, Artie started up his car and drove away. It was time to get back to the dirty business of being a cop.

The Law Office of Branch, Cornwell & Steiner was located in the heart of downtown Philadelphia. When Frank and Craig stepped off the elevator and into the large, lavish lobby, they were greeted warmly by a short, older Jewish man. They followed the man into his private office and shut the door.

"Gentlemen, it's good to see you again," Robert Steiner said as he pulled out two chairs for them to be seated. "Frank, I heard the terrible news and I'm truly sorry."

"Thank you, Robert."

"So, gentlemen, how can I be of assistance this time?" Robert asked.

"Robert, I need you to find out everything you can on a guy named Vega Littles. I need to know everything about him—family, if he owns any property, his childhood—everything!"

"Just like I did Vincent Angilino?" Robert asked with a devilish grin.

"Exactly," Frank said.

Robert saw the seriousness in Frank's eyes and nodded. "It will take some time, but give me a week or so and I'll have everything you need."

Craig reached into his pocket and pulled out a thick stack of hundred-dollar bills. He passed the money to Robert and said, "That's twenty-five grand. You'll get another twenty-five whenever you call us with the information."

Robert walked over and put the money inside his desk.

"If you don't mind telling me, who is this guy Vega Littles?" Robert asked.

"The person who's responsible for my parents' deaths," Frank said.

Robert nodded again.

"I talked to Pete earlier," Frank said as he and Craig both stood. "He'll help you with anything else you need."

After shaking hands, Robert watched as Frank and Craig walked out of his office and got back on the elevator.

The last time he had seen Frank so serious about something was the time Frank had told him to get all the info he could on Vincent Angilino. At the time Vincent Angilino was one of the top made members in the Italian mob. That was three long years ago. Since then no one had seen or heard a thing about the mysterious disappearance of Vincent Angilino, or his wife Maria, and their two young children.

Robert sat down at his desk and reached for the telephone. He had a lot of important people to call. If anyone could find out about Vega Littles, it was him. For the right price this was what he did—discover people's whereabouts and secrets. Robert was a well connected criminal lawyer, and once one of the most powerful people in the tri-state area. On a daily basis he'd brushed shoulders with men and women of great wealth and bright political futures.

But his relationship with Frank was a lot different from his past business dealings. It was Frank who provided Robert with the two things he loved most in this world—tax-free cash and a plethora of beautiful, exotic women.

Southwest Philly

"Motherfucker, I said where's all my damn money?" Butcher yelled as he looked at the beaten man who was tied to a wooden chair. The man's face was bruised and swollen beyond recognition. Blood was pouring from his nose, mouth, and both eyes. Two of Butcher's men stood around holding loaded guns. They were all inside an old warehouse on Greenway Avenue where Butcher brought all his victims. With blood all over his black gloves, Butcher punched the man in the face as hard as he could. Blood squirted everywhere.

"I told you not to play with me, didn't I?" Butcher yelled.

The man was too beaten to respond. A piece of his top lip was hanging off his face. Butcher walked over and picked up two sharp knives from the floor. When he walked back over to his victim he said, "I told you that this game ain't for everybody. And only the strong survive."

Then without any hesitation, Butcher stuck one of the knives straight through the man's neck, and he didn't pull it back out. Butcher's men stood around with shocked looks on their faces. Neither one said a word.

As the man sat there slowly dying, Butcher reached out with the other knife and stabbed the man between his eyes. Then he stood there with a smile on his face watching as his victim closed his eyes for the last time. For Butcher, death never felt so good.

CHAPTER 8

Later that night

UNDERWORLD ENTERTAINMENT WAS LOCATED IN the middle of Center City Philadelphia. The company rented space inside a high-rise office building just a few blocks away from City Hall. Underworld occupied the top two floors of the building, so whenever someone looked out the windows, they could see the entire city of Philadelphia as well as the large Benjamin Franklin Bridge that connected Philly to Camden, New Jersey

Inside one of the large conference rooms, Frank sat at the head of a long glass table. Seven people sat around listening to every word he said. Craig and Graveyard were there, as well as Meatloaf, a drug boss from North Philly, Domino, a drug boss from South Philly, Passion, a female drug dealer from West Philly, and Bingo, another drug boss from Southwest Philly.

Each of the drug dealers had one thing in common—they all worked for Frank. He was their major drug connect. Every time Frank received another shipment of drugs from his connect in Miami, these were the people he would sell to.

Juan Sanchez sent Frank between twenty-five hundred to thirty-five hundred kilos of cocaine each month, and another two hundred kilos of pure heroin. Not only did Frank supply 60 percent of Philadelphia with these drugs, but he also supplied a major part of South Jersey, Delaware, and even parts of West

Baltimore. Frank also had a few people he supplied in Brooklyn, New York and Hartford, Connecticut.

"Does anyone here know where Vega gets his drugs?" Frank asked in a calm voice.

"I do," Meatloaf said.

Frank's eyes lit up. "Who?" he asked.

"Vega gets all his drugs from a guy named Carlos Benitez. He's the boss of the Dominican cartel from North Philly," Meatloaf said. "I know everything that goes down in North Philly, and the Dominicans are my main competition."

Craig felt his two-way pager vibrating on his waist. When he checked the message, he smiled and closed it. He would have a pleasurable night, but business came first. He turned his attention back to the conversation.

"What else do you know about this guy Carlos Benitez?" Frank asked.

"I know where he and his crew like to eat breakfast," Meatloaf said. "A Spanish restaurant called Falishios Delights, right down the street from Temple University."

"What's going on? What's up?" Bingo asked, wanting to know why Frank was asking all these questions.

"What's up is that Carlos has to go! He's Vega's drug connect, so if he's out of the way, then Vega will need someone else to replace him."

"Who, us?" Domino asked with a surprised look on his face.

"No, nobody," Frank replied. "This will be the start of his crumbling organization. I don't want to just hurt 'im. I want to destroy him! And the only way to do that is to first eliminate all the people he depends on. Then I'll destroy all the people he loves."

"Underworld, when would you like this done?" Passion asked.

Underworld looked around the room at everyone's faces and said, "I want Carlos Benitez to be dead by Wednesday!"

Everyone nodded. The contract was signed and sealed. Now all that was left to do was deliver the head of Carlos Benitez.

For the next hour, Frank talked about everything that needed to be done to destroy Vega and bring down his entire organization. After the meeting ended, they all left the building, got into their expensive cars, and headed off in different directions.

FBI Special Agents Mitchell and Stokes sat inside a dark blue Ford Taurus, right across the street from the high-rise building where Underworld Entertainment was located. They watched Frank and Craig go into the building, followed by an unknown male and four of the biggest drug dealers in the city. Both agents wore excited expressions on their pale faces. They knew that something very big was about to go down.

The agents were only in the beginning stages of their FBI investigation of the Underworld drug cartel. So far all they had on Frank and his crew was some useless information from paid street informants, and a lot of unproven statements from two federal prisoners, who were trying to cut a deal with the U.S. federal prosecutor to get some time off their lengthy sentences. But with nothing solid, they were still stuck on square one. They knew that in order to get a grand jury to indict the powerful Frank "Underworld" Simms, they would need a whole lot more than some statements from two jailhouse snitches. Both agents knew that it took a lot of patience to build a case. But time didn't matter to them, because Agents Mitchell and Stokes were two men who were determined to bring down the Underworld cartel, no matter how long it took.

When the two federal agents finally pulled off down the street, they had no idea that a keen pair of eyes had been carefully watching their every move. Sitting in his car a block away, looking through a pair of night vision binoculars was Graveyard. After he went to North Philly to check out Falishios Delights, he decided to drive back by the building, and he was not glad he did just that.

Graveyard put the binoculars back into the stash spot under his seat, and slowly pulled off down the street. In the morning, the first thing he planned to do was call Frank and tell him that the feds were on him.

Inside the Dollhouse Gentlemen's social club twenty beautiful, half-dressed strippers paraded around in tiny red outfits. Men of all races stood around laughing, drinking, and tossing money in the air. Once again the place was filled to capacity. The Dollhouse was a private social club that few people knew about. Only those who needed to know knew that the owner of the establishment was one of the most ruthless drug dealers in the city. And Vega was determined to keep it that way. Vega had invested his drug money into a lot of legitimate businesses. Besides the Dollhouse, he also owned a few rental properties, two used-car dealerships, a small soul food restaurant, a pool hall, and a popular hair salon and barbershop on Germantown Avenue.

Vega had turned himself into a self-made millionaire. He had everything he ever wanted in life— everything except the two things that had constantly eluded him—the crown on Frank's head and the title of boss of the underworld.

While Vega, Junie, and Artie were all inside a back room enjoying a few beautiful strippers, Butcher and

Homicide were inside Butcher's car parked right out in front of the club.

"Here. It's a hundred fifty grand," Homicide said, passing a rolled up plastic bag to Butcher.

"Damn. We making thirty grand off each key?" Butcher asked, excited.

"Them white boys don't care. As long as it's good, they got the money to pay for it."

Butcher reached over and grabbed a backpack from the backseat. "Here. This is three kilos to hold you off. Me and Vega supposed to go re-up on Thursday," Butcher said, passing Homicide the backpack.

"All right, but the way things have been moving, I should be out in a few days."

"Don't worry, Homicide. Our Dominican connect is always there. We'll have another two hundred kilos on Thursday for sure, Underworld ain't the only person who got drugs in this city," Butcher said as they both started laughing. "Come on. Lets get back in there before Vega starts wondering where we ran off to."

When Butcher and Homicide walked back into the private room, Vega, Artie, and Junie were all inside enjoying lap dances. As reggae music blasted from the large speakers, they all sat around enjoying themselves.

Around one thirty-five AM, Butcher, Artie, Vega, and Junie all left the club. Butcher had two beautiful strippers with him. They climbed into his Lexus and headed for the Holiday Inn. Artie also had one of the strippers with him, but instead of spending his money on a hotel room, he found a dark, quiet spot behind an old, broken down gas station. Unlike his friend Butcher, Artie had a wife and three children at home.

Junie dropped off Vega at home and watched him walk into the house. Once Vega was safely inside, Junie drove off down the street.

When Vega walked into his bedroom, Raquel was sleeping in bed with their six-year-old daughter Erika snuggled under her arms. Vega shut the door and walked down the hallway to a backroom. Inside the room were a small table and a leather chair. Lying on top of the table was a large green duffel bag. Vega dumped the contents of the bag onto the table. Stacks of money covered the entire table. He reached under the table and grabbed his electric money counting and started counting. In a few more days it would be time for him to re-up with his drug connect, Mr. Carlos Benitez, the notorious drug lord of the Dominican cartel.

Delaware Avenue

Craig parked his Mercedes Benz and walked into the elegant, well furnished lobby of his high-rise condominium. The thirty-story condominium high-rise was one of the new buildings erected along the Delaware River waterfront. The condos started at a quarter million dollars, and they were selling like hotcakes. Craig was one of the first people to purchase his, but now most of the building was full.

When Craig stepped off the elevator he walked over to his door and let himself inside. His plush condo was elegant from top to bottom. It had a large, freshwater fish tank built into the wall, a gold chandelier hanging from the ceiling, and a huge, beige leather sectional filling the main room. Plush wall-to-wall carpet, a grand piano, and a large outdoor balcony completed the main living area.

Craig walked to his master bedroom and opened the door. He just stood there for a moment with a big smile on his face. The beautiful, naked woman that was lying across his king-sized bed was none other than twenty-six-year-old R&B singing sensation, Janell Jones, one of the most successful recording artists in the entire world. Her latest song called "Love Can't Wait" was currently number one on the R&B charts and number seven on the pop charts. In her short five-year career, Janell had released four multi-platinum albums, selling over twelve million copies worldwide.

Not only did Janell have an exceptional voice, but she was also an extremely beautiful woman. Her light brown caramel complexion and long, silky hair accented her God-given beauty. She could sing, dance, and act with the best of them. Born and raised in Harlem, Janell was discovered one day by music legend Clive Davis, the founder of J Records. After Clive signed the gifted young singer to his record label, she became an instant success and never looked back.

"So what brings you back to Philly?" Craig asked as he started unbuttoning his shirt.

"You, handsome, always you," Janell said in low, sexy voice.

"So how did you manage to get away from that overprotective manager of yours?"

"I snuck away, but I'm sure he knows where I'm at. There's only one man in this world who keeps me running back to him," Janell said with a smile.

"No MTV, BET, or music award shows this week?" Craig asked as he stood there sliding down his pants.

"Nope. I start my national tour in twenty days, but tonight I'm totally free. And overdue," Janell teased.

"What about that handsome new actor you're supposed to be dating?" Craig asked while sliding down his boxers.

"Who? John Stenton? Please, he's gayer than Little Richard," Janell said as they both started laughing.

"But I've seen y'all on a few of those celebrity gossip magazines all hugged up like two young lost lovers."

"That's because my publicist and agent set that up. It's all promotional, a way to blow up our careers even more and stay in the spotlight. It's all fake, just like most of Hollywood is."

Craig stood there in front of her wearing nothing. Janell looked at his gorgeous body and well endowed manhood and started licking her lips.

"You know you can get into a lot of trouble if you ever get caught with me," Craig said, climbing on top of the bed.

"Well it's been going on for almost two years, and we haven't gotten caught yet," Janell said as she started rubbing her soft, manicured hands across his naked body. "I can't help it, Craig, if you got me sprung. As long as you keep doing what you do, I'll keep cumming . . . and coming back," Janell said and giggled.

Janell climbed on top of Craig's body and started passionately kissing him. She then reached under one of the six fluffy pillows and pulled out a Magnum condom. She sat up and looked into Craig's eyes.

"I bought you a new box of these," she said as she ripped the wrapper open with her mouth and took out the condom. After sliding the large condom over Craig's rock hard dick, Janell started to lick and kiss all over his body. Behind closed doors, the beautiful superstar was a cold freak. Whenever she got with her secret lover, they did any and everything. There were no limits to their lovemaking.

After kissing all over Craig's body, Janell climbed on top of him and stared into his sexy brown eyes. "You know I be singing about you in my new song, right?" she asked.

"I hope so," Craig said and smiled.

Janell put her lips to his ear and started singing. "Baby, I miss you so much, yearning desperately for your gentle touch, wishing that you were here, deep, so deep inside of me, my love can't wait any longer, my love can't wait."

Once again they started passionately kissing. Then in one smooth motion Janell grabbed Craig's rock hard dick and slid it into her wet, warm paradise as far as it could go. In the tranquility of the bedroom they started making love to each other like there was no tomorrow.

CHAPTER 9

Chestnut Hill

WHEN FRANK WALKED INTO HIS home all the lights were off except for a small lamp that sat on top of a table next to the sofa. With his cell phone in his hand, Frank headed up the stairs. After opening the door to his bedroom, Frank just stood there with a smile on his face. Cassie lay in the bed sleeping peacefully with a silk sheet covering her body. Frank turned around and tiptoed out of the room. He quietly closed the door and walked back downstairs.

Frank sat down on the sofa and kicked up both of his legs. For a few moments he sat there thinking about the day's events. A lot was on his mind, but nothing more pressing than seeing his dead parents lying in the morgue. That was a sight that Frank would never forget as long as he lived.

Looking at his gold Rolex watch, he saw that it was twelve thirteen in the morning. He started dialing a number on his cell phone. After four rings, a male's voice finally answered.

"Hello? Who's this?" the man asked.

"It's me, Underworld," Frank said.

"Oh, what's up, Underworld? I haven't heard from you in a while," the man said.

"I need you again, Cooper. It's very important."

"How can I help this time?"

"Do you know a Spanish restaurant called Falishios Delights?"

"Yeah, I drive by it all the time while I'm working. I ate there a few times. The burritos are excellent. Why? What's up?"

"How would you like to make the fastest twenty grand that you ever made in your life?"

"I'm all ears, Underworld. Run it down," Cooper said, giving Frank his full attention.

After Frank ran down everything, he closed his cell phone and laid it on the coffee table. His plan was slowly coming together. Frank had a lot of friends that would do almost anything he asked. Cooper was one of them.

Once again Frank started thinking about his dead parents. He couldn't get the vision of them lying in the morgue out of his mind. Suddenly tears started falling from his eyes.

Tuesday

Craig opened his eyes and looked around his empty bedroom. The silk sheets and pillows were scattered all over the bed from the wild night of sex that he had with Janell. Craig looked over at the nightstand and noticed a white piece of paper lying on top of it. He reached out and grabbed it. Then he sat up and started reading.

HEY, HANDSOME, I DIDN'T WANT TO WAKE YOU, BECAUSE WHEN YOU'RE ASLEEP YOU SEEM SO MUCH AT PEACE. LAST NIGHT WAS WONDERFUL! BELIEVE ME, I REALLY NEEDED THAT. TO BE HONEST, I KNOW HOW BAD YOU NEEDED TO RELIEVE SOME STRESS TOO. I HEARD ABOUT FRANK'S PARENTS, AND I KNOW HOW MUCH THEY MEANT TO YOU. THAT'S WHY I LEFT NEW YORK AS SOON AS POSSIBLE AND HURRIED TO PHILLY. EVEN IF IT WAS FOR

ONE NIGHT ONLY, I WANTED TO BE THE SHOULDER YOU COULD LEAN ON. CRAIG, I WANT YOU TO KNOW THAT I THINK ABOUT YOU OFTEN. AND AFTER LAST NIGHT'S PERFORMANCE, I'LL BE SENDING YOU OUT THE BILL FOR MY SORE BACK. SMILE. I LOVE THIS RELATIONSHIP WE HAVE. MAYBE ONE DAY WE CAN EXPLORE IT MORE. WHEN I FIRST MET YOU BACKSTAGE AT THE BET AWARDS TWO YEARS AGO, I KNEW FROM LOOKING INTO YOUR SEXY BROWN EYES THAT THERE WAS SOMETHING SPECIAL ABOUT YOU. AND MY FEMALE INTUITION WASN'T WRONG. PLEASE BE SAFE OUT THERE. I DON'T KNOW WHAT I WOULD DO IF ANYTHING WAS EVER TO HAPPEN TO YOU. DON'T HESITATE TO CALL ME IF YOU NEED ME. FOR YOU, I'M ALWAYS JUST ONE PHONE CALL AWAY. AND BELIEVE ME WHEN I TELL YOU, MY LOVE CAN'T WAIT.
LOVE ALWAYS, JANELL

Craig set the piece of paper back down and smiled. As he stood from his bed, he thought about the strange relationship he had with Janell. She was the only woman that had a key to his condo. And it seemed like every time he needed someone to be there, Janell always found a way to show up.

After stretching, Craig walked into the walk-in shower. The scent of Janell was still on his naked body. And the wonderful thoughts of last night were still lingering inside his mind.

Deacon Harris was sitting on the sofa in his living room when his wife Nora walked downstairs. The first thing that she noticed were the stacks of hundred-dollar bills laid out neatly across the coffee table. Deacon Harris quickly grabbed the money and started putting it inside a small brown bag.

"Honey, where did you get all that money?" Nora asked with a shocked look on her face.

"It's nothing, dear. I did a favor for someone and they paid me for it," Deacon Harris said, then stood up from the sofa.

Nora looked into her husband's eyes and saw nervousness written all over his face. For the last few days she had noticed a major change in him.

"Honey, is everything all right?" she asked.

"I'm fine, love. Just got a lot on my mind," Deacon Harris said as he walked up and kissed her.

"Can I do anything to help you?"

"Just pray for my sins, and let the man above do the rest," he said before walking over to the door and rushing out of the house.

Later that afternoon
Underworld Entertainment

Cassie was sitting inside her office when a tall, black man tapped on the door, then stepped inside.

"Riley, what is it?" she asked, turning away from her computer.

"Ms. Lopez, will the boss be in today?"

"No, he won't be at work all this week. How can I help you?" Cassie asked, folding her arms across her chest.

"Today the boss was supposed to do an interview and photo shoot with *VIBE* magazine. I've been trying to call him all morning. I even tried to call Craig. He's not answering his cell phone either," Riley said.

"Oh, hell, I forgot all about his interview with *VIBE*," Cassie replied as she stood from her chair. "Where are they?"

"The *VIBE* staff writer and a photographer are out in the lobby," Riley said.

"Well I need you to go back and tell then that due to the sudden passing of Frank's parents, he'd really appreciate it if they would consider doing the interview at a later time. Now go do it," Cassie ordered.

Riley turned to walk out the door, then paused. He turned back around and said, "Ms. Lopez, do you want me to call all the others and tell 'em the same thing?"

"Who are all the others?" Cassie asked as she sat back down at her computer desk.

"Well this week the boss was supposed to meet with *XXL*, *The Source*, Russell Simmons, *GQ* magazine, and the people at BET."

After a long sigh, Cassie looked at Riley and said, "Just tell 'em all the same thing, Riley. Your Frank's personal assistant, so get on out there and go earn your damn money!" Without saying another word, Riley rushed out of the office and closed the door.

Yeadon, PA

Inside his black tinted BMW, Frank sat alone, watching the large truck drive into his private warehouse. The warehouse was surrounded by a tall, barbed-wire fence. Craig was also there, inside his Mercedes, which was parked around the back of the warehouse. As two large men stood around on lookout, a truck entered the huge warehouse and one of the men quickly shut and locked the gate behind it. A few moments later Frank's cell phone started ringing.

"Yo!" he answered.

"It's all here. We're unloading now," the man's voice said.

Without saying another word, Frank closed his phone. Even though the phones they used were all untraceable, Frank still didn't like to talk any kind of business on them.

Inside the warehouse, five of Frank's men were unloading twenty-five hundred kilos of cocaine and two hundred kilos of pure heroin. Forty-five minutes later, Frank watched as the truck drove out of the warehouse. Then one of Frank's workers rushed out and locked the gate. The shipment from Miami was worth thirty million dollars in street value, so keeping it secure was paramount.

When Frank pulled off, Craig was right behind him. A few streets down, a Yeadon police car pulled up right behind Craig's Mercedes. The officer followed behind both cars until they had safely reached the city limits. Once both cars had crossed back into Philly, the officer waved and turned his police car back around.

City Line Avenue

When Vega saw his white Cadillac Escalade pull up in front of his house and park, he walked over to Raquel and gave her a warm hug. Erika ran down the stairs and joined in.

"Will you be late tonight?" Raquel asked.

"Probably so. I have a lot of things to take care of today," Vega said.

"Oh, Daddy, you promised us pizza and a movie," Erika said, frowning.

"As soon as Daddy finds time, sweetie, I promise, me, you, and mommy will have our pizza and sit back and enjoy a nice movie together."

Raquel was surprised at Vega's promise. He had never made those types of promises to their daughter before. She looked into Vega's eyes and said, "I don't know what's gotten into you lately, but ever since Sunday you have become a changed man."

"That's because I released a lot of deep down anger that was bottled up inside me for too many years," Vega replied.

Raquel and Erika watched as Vega walked out of the house and got into the truck. As soon he shut the truck door, Junie pulled off down the street.

Vega looked over at Junie with a serious expression on his face. Junie could tell that something was on his mind.

"What is it?" Junie asked.

"Unc, do you think if my parents were still alive, they would be proud of me?" Vega asked.

Junie pulled over to the side of the road and double parked. He needed to make sure he addressed Vega's question with his full attention. "Vega, my sister loved you. When she first laid eyes on you, she begged her husband to adopt you. They both loved you more than anything in this world. I still remember when they first brought you home. You weren't even a full year yet. They showed you off to everybody, and felt good giving you their last name. When they died in that car accident three years ago, I know that they both truly loved you. And to answer your question, yes, they would both be proud of you."

"Unc, I have something very personal to tell you."

"What?"

"A deep secret that I've kept to myself for three years now," Vega said.

"Does Raquel know?"

"Nobody."

"Well, what is it?" Junie asked curiously.

Vega looked into his uncle's eyes and began telling him his deepest and most personal secret. For three long years Vega had kept this secret all to himself. And now he was revealing it to someone for the first time.

"That's why I did it, Unc," Vega said when he had finished revealing his secret. "This is so much bigger than Tony."

Junie sat there with a look of total disbelief on his face. He still couldn't believe what he had just heard. Not in a million years could he ever imagine what Vega had just told him. His mind was racing with thoughts.

"Damn!" was all Junie could say.

After a long sigh, Junie looked deep into Vega's serious eyes and shook his head. When he pulled off down the street, neither man said another word.

CHAPTER 10

Manhattan

INSIDE HER LUXURIOUS SUITE AT the Waldorf-Astoria Hotel, Janell was getting her face made up by her own personal makeup artist. Her hair, nails, and toes had already been done. Janell was seated on a wooden stool, dressed in a white Baby Phat blouse, a pair of black DKNY jeans, and white Jimmy Choo wrap-around sandals. The door to her room swung open and her manager Joe walked into the room.

"Laura, can you leave us alone for a few minutes?" he asked the makeup artist.

Laura set down her makeup kit on the counter and walked out the room.

"Please don't start, Joe," Janell said, already knowing what he was about to say.

"What do you mean don't start! You're a multi-platinum music artist, one of the most successful females in the music industry, and every chance you get, you sneak off to Philadelphia to be with some street thug," Joe vented.

"Joe, Craig is not a thug," Janell said, folding her arms across her chest.

"Will you stop kidding yourself? Everyone in the industry knows about those people at Underworld Entertainment. I'm sure you heard the rumors."

"Just like all rumors about me and Usher, and me and Eve, and Missy and everybody else. They're all lies."

Joe walked up to Janell and looked straight into her eyes. "Janell, sweetie, you have one of the most recognized faces in the world. You have a large fan base that respects you. Do you know what will happen to your career if the press got a hold of some photos with you and Craig together? All I'm saying, Janell, is to think about it. I know you like this guy, but—"

"No, Joe, you're wrong!" Janell said, cutting him off. "What I feel for Craig is way more than like. See, Craig is not fake like so many of these superficial celebrities. The reason why we both get along is because we are both from the same place—the ghetto, something that you know nothing about. When I'm with Craig it's the only time I can truly be myself. That's why once in a while I need to escape this fake ass world I'm living in and run to reality. I don't care what you say, Joe, and I don't care how many CDs I stop selling if the press finds out about my relationship with Craig. I have very strong feelings for Craig, and there ain't nothing you, the label, or anyone else can do about it," Janell said as she stood from the stool and walked over to the door.

"Look, Joe, I have to go do this *Essence* interview and photo shoot, then we have to fly out to L.A. to meet up with Denzel's people about me getting that lead roll in his next movie. You're my manager and I appreciate everything you've done for my career, but from now on please let me worry about my private life," Janell said as she turned and walked out of the room.

After a long sigh, Joe shook his head and disappointingly followed behind her.

Thirty-ninth Street, West Philly

The two FBI agents sat inside an all-white van, watching the traffic that was going in and out of a small house. As they sat watching the entire street, they couldn't believe all the drug activity that was taking place. Crackheads were coming and going like zombies. People were pulling up in cars and paying for the best drugs that money could buy—cocaine, marijuana, dope, pills, and whatever else they used to get high. Thirty-ninth Street was one of many streets in Philadelphia that had it all. The neighborhood that Thirty-ninth Street was located in was known as the bottom. Drugs, violence, and crime were the way of life for most of the people who lived around this poverty-stricken community.

The two agents had watched Butcher come to the house four times in the last hour. After seeing what they needed to see, they pulled off in the van and headed downtown to the FBI's main office.

Inside Cassie's office, Cassie and Riley stood around listening to the complaints of one of their top-selling rap artists, a talented young rapper from Brooklyn, New York. J-Dawg's last two albums were both certified platinum. He was a nineteen-year-old rapping phenomenon whose lyrical skills were being compared to some of the New York's finest MCs— Biggie, Jay-Z, and Nas. The bidding war with Def Jam and Interscope records had cost Frank over a million dollars. But like always, in the end Frank and his Underworld Entertainment Company had come out on top.

"Cassie, I need more money for my video budget!" J-Dawg said as he stood there dressed in the latest Sean

John fashions, Air Force Ones, and iced out platinum jewelry that lit up his neck, ears, and wrists.

Cassie looked over at Riley and shook her head. She knew J-Dawg was never satisfied. They'd had this same discussion so many times before.

"J-Dawg, we have spent over a million dollars on each of your last two videos," Cassie began. "I have personally made sure you had the top music director and video girls in the industry. I'm really getting tired of all your shit! A year and a half ago you were a broke ass, high school dropout, rapping for free. And now because of us your family is set for life, and so are you. You have two more albums to give us, and then you can do what the hell you want after that. But if you don't turn your ass around and get out of my office with this nonsense, I'll rip up that damn contract and do everything in my power to make sure you never make another penny in this industry!"

J-Dawg looked over at Riley, who was standing there smiling with his arms crossed. J-Dawg then turned to Cassie and said, "You are one tough broad."

Then he turned and walked out of the office. When J-Dawg shut the door behind himself, Cassie and Riley both busted out laughing.

Downtown Philadelphia

Robert Steiner sat at his desk gathering up all the information he had found on Vega Littles. He had been working nonstop ever since Frank visited his office. Robert had called all of his inside sources, and with each call he was learning more and more about Vega Littles. Being in the powerful Philadelphia circle truly had its advantages. And Robert was a sharp, old, Jewish lawyer who knew how to get whatever it was he needed.

Robert had been receiving faxes and text messages about Vega all morning long. In a few more days he would have almost every piece of information available on Vega Littles. Then once he passed that information on to Frank, another twenty-five thousand dollars in cash would be waiting for him.

After Robert hung up the phone with Pete Childs, the assistant DA, and another close friend of Frank's, he reached for his telephone and dialed Frank's cell phone number. Frank picked up after the first ring.

"Hello?"

"Frank, it's me, Robert. I just wanted to let you know that I'm getting everything together for you. And from the way things are going, I should be ready for you sooner than you think."

"Good work, Robert."

"Um, Frank . . . Frank?"

"Yeah, Robert, spit it out," Frank said with a smile on his face.

He already knew what else it was that Robert wanted. Frank made a habit to keep all of his friends close. And know about all of their strengths, weaknesses, and dark secrets.

"Um . . . Frank . . . um . . ."

"Robert, are you gonna say it? I'm on my way to meet a few people, so spit it out or I'm going to hang up the phone," Frank said, turning his BMW down Belmont Avenue, headed toward Fairmount Park.

"Frank, can you send over DNA? It's been a little over a month, and me and my wife—"

"What time?" Frank asked, cutting him off in mid speech.

"How about nine o'clock?"

"They'll be there. Bye, Robert," Frank said before pressing the end button.

Robert smiled, then turned to his computer and went back to work.

After Frank made the call for Robert, he closed his cell phone and tossed it on the empty passenger seat. As he drove through beautiful Fairmount Park, he looked into his rearview mirror and saw Craig's Mercedes Benz right behind him. And right behind Craig was Graveyard, cruising inside the black Dodge Magnum. When their cars pulled up at the Belmont Plateau, there were four other cars parked next to each other waiting. Meatloaf, Domino, Passion, and Bingo all got out of their cars. After Frank parked his car, and Craig and Graveyard did the same, they all exited their vehicles. Everybody shook hands and gave warm hugs before saying a word.

This was Frank's crew. Each person had been hand picked by him personally. They were loyal, street smart, and true friends—three qualities that Frank put over all others. Especially loyalty. Frank knew that in order to survive in this game, a person of his power needed men and women of loyalty inside his circle. Without loyalty from his soldiers, a king and his kingdom would surely crumble, usually from the betrayal of one of his own men. That was why Frank played the game of life like a chess game, making strategic advance moves and surrounding himself with powerful pawns, bishops, knights, rooks, and queens.

"Meatloaf, did you go check that out?" Frank asked, getting straight to business.

"Yeah, Underworld, me and Passion went by there this morning. We saw Carlos and two of his men at a back table laughing, but they never saw us. I also met with Cooper early this morning. I took care of him, and now everything is straight."

"Good. Graveyard will meet y'all on the corner of Broad and Master at nine. Y'all know what to do from there."

Everyone nodded.

"Also, that new shipment came this morning. Each of y'all will get two hundred kilos delivered to your stash house in an hour. So make sure everything is secured for the delivery. Remember, it only takes one mistake in this game to cost us. We can't afford any," Frank said in a serious voice. "Anybody have anything to say?" No one said a word.

After everyone hugged and shook hands again, Frank watched as Bingo, Meatloaf, Domino, and Passion all got into their expensive cars and drove away.

"Why didn't you tell them about the feds being on us?" Craig asked.

"Because I don't want to concern them with something that's minor," Frank said.

"The feds ain't got nothing. If they did, I would've known forty-eight hours before they did," Frank said confidently.

Both Craig and Graveyard stood around groaning and shaking their heads. They knew that Frank wasn't being cocky or arrogant, but just telling the truth. Frank had so many powerful people in his pocket that he was considered untouchable.

"What's next?" Craig asked.

"I need you to call Tadpole in Baltimore and tell 'im that shipment of heroin will be there later tonight," Frank said while getting inside his BMW. "I'll see you later."

"Where are you going now?" Craig asked.

"I'm going back home. I have a lot on my mind," Frank said as he started up his car and slowly pulled off down the road.

Later that evening

Inside the house in Southwest Philly, Vega had just finished another round of wild sex with Jewell and Cindy. After putting on his black silk robe, he slid into his slippers and walked downstairs. Waiting downstairs in the living room were Junie, Butcher, and his two young assassins, Canon and Spade. Vega walked over and sat down on the sofa. Then he lifted his feet to the coffee table and put his hands behind his head.

When Vega looked up, he noticed Spade standing there with a large green snake wrapped around her neck. "Spade, keep that damn snake away from me," Vega said. "You know I can't stand them damn things!"

"I never knew that," she said, taking a step back.

"Well now you do! I hate them bastards!"

Vega looked around all the faces in the room and said,

"Where's Homicide?"

"He's down at the club making sure everything is in order," Butcher replied.

"What about Artie?"

"He called about twenty minutes ago, said he had to take care of some business at the police station," Junie said.

"Well I called everyone to let y'all know about the next few moves we'll be making." Vega looked at Canon and Spade and said, "The Deacon has got to go next. He knows too much."

Spade and Canon both beamed. Another name to add to their long list of executions.

"When would you like this done, boss?" Canon asked as he rubbed his hand on the snake around Spade's neck.

"Monday y'all can go by the church and take care of that," Vega said, looking at the strange couple.

"Junie will have everything y'all need."

"What about Underworld?" Butcher asked.

"Well next Tuesday is the big rap concert at the Civic Center. Underworld Entertainment will have a few of their artists performing at the show. So Frank, Craig, and Cassie will all be there. I'll make sure I have everyone inside and out positioned and ready to kill any of them on sight."

"And where will you be?" Butcher asked.

"Right here upstairs fucking my two beauties," Vega said as everyone started laughing. "I'll let Homicide and Artie know about everything in the morning," Vega said.

"Boss, did you get with your man Carlos?" Butcher asked.

"Yeah, I talked with him earlier. He'll be ready for us on Thursday. Everything is set."

"Good, 'cause we're almost finished. The drug spots have been moving like crazy," Butcher said.

"Don't worry, Butcher, everything will be taken care of," Vega said as he stood from the sofa. "I'll see you tomorrow. And, Spade?"

"Yeah, boss," she answered in a sweet, innocent voice.

"The next time you come over here, leave that damn snake at home."

"Sure will," she said, rubbing her snake and following Junie, Canon, and Butcher out the front door.

After everyone left, Vega headed back upstairs to his beautiful young nymphs.

Chapter 11

Chestnut Hill, Philadelphia

WHEN CASSIE WALKED INTO THE house she saw Frank sitting on the sofa staring at an old photo of his deceased parents. Cassie laid her Prada Bag and Blackberry on a table, walked over to Frank, and sat down beside him. She looked into his eyes and could see that Frank had been crying. She reached out and gave him a loving hug. The tears started falling from both of their eyes.

"I can't believe they're gone," Frank said as he laid the picture on the coffee table. "And it's all my fault!"

"Frank, don't do this to yourself, baby," Cassie said. "You can't just take the blame for something that someone else is responsible for. Vega was behind this. He and his crew are the people who are responsible for killing your parents."

"Yeah, but they wanted me! I'm who they want, Cassie! My parents are dead now because of me and the choices I've made."

Cassie sat there shaking her head. She knew that Frank was speaking the truth.

"I chose this life, Cassie! And it cost them theirs. And there is nothing I could ever do to bring them back. Nothing!" Frank shouted.

"Please, Frank, please don't do this to yourself. We have to move on from this tragedy. We've done it before. We can do it again!"

Frank looked deep into Cassie's watery eyes and said, "My parents' funeral is Friday. How can I look at their dead bodies knowing that I'm the main reason they're lying in caskets? How?"

"By doing what you've always done—facing your fears instead of running away from them. And Friday you and I will look at them together, side by side, just like they would've wanted us to," Cassie said, grabbing his hand. "We are in this together, baby. Your pain is my pain, but you know just as much as I do that now it's time for us to move on. Your parents are with God now, and one of these days the four of us will all be together again."

After a long sigh, Frank looked at Cassie and cracked a smile. She was his strength and backbone, the only woman he could ever see himself with. Her genuine spirit was the reason he had fallen in love with her. Cassie was one of those rare women who possessed beauty, brains, and a loving soul. She was an angel that was sent straight from God himself. She had been by Frank's side through thick and thin, and was determined to stay there forever.

In the tranquility of their lovely home, Frank and Cassie cried in each other's arms. As they sat there holding each other, an aura of unconditional love surrounded them both.

Baltimore, Maryland

Tadpole and one of his men sat inside a black Chevy Suburban in front of a small row house in West Baltimore. Suddenly a gray Toyota Camry drove down the street and parked behind the Suburban. A young black man dressed in a pizza delivery outfit got out of the car holding two large brown bags in his hands. He quickly walked over to the truck and got inside.

"This is from Underworld," the man said. "I got five more bags in the trunk." After he unloaded all five bags from the trunk, the man got back into his car and sped off down the dark street. Moments later, the Chevy Suburban slowly pulled off in the opposite direction.

Antonio "Tadpole" Simms was Frank's twenty-six-year-old cousin. He had been working with Frank for three years, flooding the cities of Baltimore and Washington D.C. with the best dope on East Coast. Just like the rest of Frank's men, Tadpole was a loyal and dependable soldier, one that would rather die than cause his favorite older cousin any harm.

Philadelphia, PA, The Marriott Hotel

Inside his cozy downtown hotel room, Graveyard lay across the bed, deep in thought. In the morning he had a very important job to do, and he wanted it to go as smoothly as possible. As he lay on the bed staring up at the ceiling, a soft knock at the door interrupted his peaceful zone. Graveyard got up and grabbed his loaded 9 mm pistol with a silencer attached. He walked over to the door, and after looking out the small peephole, he placed his gun inside his pants and opened the door.

Passion stood there dressed in a red Dolce & Gabbana dress that complemented her hour glass figure. She wore a pair of D&G heels and carried a matching red purse. After she walked inside the room, Graveyard closed the door behind her. Without exchanging any words, the two began kissing passionately. For over a year they had been secretly seeing each other. In fact, Passion had visited Graveyard a few times back in his hometown of Cleveland. There was something about his mysterious bad boy demeanor that attracted her. No one knew about their secret relationship, and that was the way they wanted to keep it.

In one smooth motion, Graveyard picked up Passion and carried her over to the bed.

Later that night

Craig walked off the balcony of his condominium and back into the spacious living room. Once again he was home alone, but it was something that he had gotten used to. Dressed in a pair of gray gym shorts and a white tank top, Craig walked over to the built-in entertainment system and found the CD he was searching for. He looked at Janell's beautiful face on the front cover and smiled. After he put in the CD, Craig walked over to the leather sofa and got comfortable. He grabbed the remote control from the coffee table and pressed play. The music came to life, and the lovely thought of Janell that had been lingering inside his mind all day long blossomed. As he sat on the sofa deep in thought, he let her beautiful, soulful voice take him to a place of tranquility. Listening to the song "Love Can't Wait" had him missing her more than ever before.

Germantown, Philadelphia

Inside his bedroom, Robert stood across from his fifty-two-year-old wife, Emily, watching as a beautiful, young black female fucked his wife from behind with an eight-inch strap-on dildo. At the same time, another beautiful, black woman who was young enough to be Robert's daughter was delivering the best oral pleasure he had ever received in his fifty-six years on earth. A third attractive black woman stood behind Robert kissing his neck. The three beautiful women were Diana, Nancy, and Adrian, better known as DNA.

The three strippers were on Frank's unlimited payroll. Whatever Frank needed them to do, they did without hesitation. The house they lived in, and the three new cars they each drove were all gifts from Frank. In return, they kept their ears to the streets and made sure Frank knew everything that was going on. They were also involved in kidnappings, murders, and providing sexual favors for some of Frank's high-class political friends like Robert and his wife Emily. Everybody had a price, and Frank knew just how to pay it. The three women stayed on call for Frank twenty-four hours a day. When the lovely ladies weren't stripping or doing a favor for Frank, they spent their time as honor roll sophomores at Temple University.

While Emily was still being fucked by Diana, Robert laid Nancy on her back and dove into her wetness. Her moans and screams were all fake, but she knew the game well. It was a game that they all had mastered perfectly. They knew that a satisfied customer always came back for more.

CHAPTER 12

Wednesday morning

ON THE CORNER OF BROAD and Master, Meatloaf, Graveyard, and Passion went over everything once more before they climbed into an old, gray Buick Regal and headed toward Falishios Delights restaurant. After Meatloaf pulled up and parked the car across the street from the restaurant, Graveyard and Passion both got out. Meatloaf sat behind the wheel, watching as Passion and Graveyard entered the restaurant. As soon as they walked inside, they sat down at a small, empty table in the back.

Carlos Benitez and two of his men sat at nearby table laughing and talking in Spanish. The restaurant was half full as the two young waitresses walked around taking orders and passing out small menus.

After one of the waitresses passed Passion a menu, she turned and rushed away. Passion and Graveyard were both wearing black shades, but no one paid their strange appearance any mind. Everyone inside the restaurant was too caught up in their own conversations to take any notice. Suddenly two black men rushed through the door waving guns.

"Everybody get the fuck down on the floor!" one of the men shouted. Both men were dressed in all black with black ski masks covering their faces.

Everyone inside the restaurant did as they were told, and quickly got down on the floor. The two men stood there with their backs against each other, making sure that no one tried anything stupid and got shot. Graveyard and Passion were both on the floor, looking over at Carlos and his two men. Inside their hands were loaded 9 mm guns with attached silencers.

While everyone in the restaurant was focused on the two masked gunmen, Graveyard and Passion had their weapons aimed at Carlos's and his two men's heads.

"Fuck this spot, man!" one of the masked men shouted. "Let's get up out of here!"

When Graveyard and Passion heard the words "Let's get up out of here," they both started firing silent, deadly shots at Carlos and his two bodyguards. The distraction had worked perfectly, and now Carlos Benitez and two of his men lay dead in small puddles of their own blood.

After the two masked men ran out of the restaurant, everyone got up and stood around in total shock. The two men didn't ask for any money and didn't harm a single soul. All they did was burst through the door, brandish their weapons, and run back out of the restaurant. The people in the restaurant finally started moving and they all rushed over to the front door, but the two masked men were now long gone. In the midst of the confusion, Graveyard and Passion calmly walked through the stunned crowd, exited the restaurant, and disappeared down the crowded street.

A block away they saw a Philadelphia police car and quickly opened the back door and got inside.

"What's up, Cooper?" Passion asked.

"Same old shit," Cooper said as he pulled off down the street. "I already dropped off Bingo and Domino at their cars. Did y'all take care of everything?" he asked as he drove down Broad Street.

"Yeah, it's a wrap," Passion answered.

When Cooper pulled his police car up to the corner of Broad and Master, Bingo, Domino, and Meatloaf were all standing around wearing different clothes.

After Cooper dropped off Passion and Graveyard, he turned his patrol car back around and headed back toward Broad Street. Moments later, everyone got back into their cars and drove off in different directions. The triple homicide had gone off perfectly. The murders worked out just like Frank and Craig had planned.

When the crowd started walking back to their seats, they all noticed the three men that were still lying on the floor. One of the waitresses walked over and saw the pools of blood that surrounded the three dead bodies.

"Ahhhhhhh! They're dead!" she screamed.

A crowd of people quickly gathered around the three dead bodies. No one could believe their eyes. No one inside the restaurant had a single clue of what happened. Both waitresses had forgotten all about the young man and woman who wore the dark shades. So many people had walked in and out of the restaurant that they couldn't remember them even if someone had asked.

Officer Roy Cooper sat inside his patrol car enjoying a glazed donut and a hot cup of coffee. When he heard a call come in on his radio about some people at a restaurant being shot, he sat there for a moment with a big smile on his face. He knew the culprits were long gone and no one would ever know who was involved. Officer Cooper was another loyal person on Frank's payroll, just like so many others around the city of Philadelphia.

After finishing his donut and coffee, Cooper started up his car and headed toward the scene of the crime while thinking about the fastest twenty grand that he had ever made. When he pulled his patrol car up to the restaurant, two other police cars and an ambulance were parked out front. There was a large crowd gathered outside the popular Spanish restaurant. Cooper got out of his patrol car and walked over to a tall, white officer.

"Tom, what the hell happened?" Cooper asked.

"Coop, we got us three dead men in the back of the restaurant. And one of them is Carlos Benitez, the boss of the Dominican mob. And what's strange is no one in the restaurant heard or saw a damn thing."

"Is that right?" Cooper asked, looking completely surprised.

One hour later

Frank's black BMW and Craig's gray S-600 Mercedes Benz were parked next to each other by the pier near Penns Landing. They stood in front of their cars talking. A black Dodge Magnum pulled up and parked beside the Mercedes, and Graveyard got out of the car and approached both men. Frank nodded. He knew that his plan would work. It was the same strategic distraction that the U.S. government and the Mafia used to assassinate President John F. Kennedy.

Frank sat on the hood of his car and crossed his arms. "Soon we'll have everything we need to know about Vega Littles. And that's when the rest of the plan will go into full effect," Frank said.

"What about the feds following us around?" Craig asked.

"Don't worry about them. They'll be dealt with sooner than you think," Frank replied.

"So you want us to continue to stay away from the company?" Craig asked.

"Yeah, at least until all this is over and done with. I don't want to bring the company any unnecessary attention. Cassie and Riley can handle things while we're gone."

"I need a few more items," Graveyard said.

"Yes?" Frank asked.

"I need some duct tape, a few pairs of handcuffs, and some thick rope. I'm also gonna need a few black vans with tinted window."

"No problem. Craig will make sure you have everything you need in a few hours," Frank said as he stood.

"Anything else, Graveyard?" Craig asked.

"Yeah, I need the money to pay the three cemetery workers. They already started digging." He grinned devilishly.

"Don't you worry, Graveyard. You'll have everything as soon as we leave here. I'm on it," Craig told him.

"Then I'll see you later. I'm going back by the cemetery, and then straight back to my hotel room," Graveyard said before getting inside his car. Frank and Craig watched as Graveyard started up the car and slowly pulled off.

"We picked the perfect man for the job," Craig said with a smile.

"I know. Let's just hope Passion don't sex him to death before he gets to finish," Frank said as he and Craig both started laughing.

After hugging and shaking hands, they both got back into their expensive cars and pulled off down the street. As he drove, Frank opened the glove compartment and took out a picture of his deceased parents. Once again tears started falling from his eyes.

Later that afternoon, Southwest Philly

"So next week we'll start our next attack!" Vega said. "The rap concert will be the perfect opportunity to catch Frank, Craig, and Cassie slipping. Homicide, you and Artie will be stationed outside the Civic Center. One of y'all will be in the front while the others will be around back. Y'all will all have walkie-talkies to communicate."

"Where are Spade and Canon?" Artie asked.

"Probably at home, staring at each other with the damn snake crawling around them," Vega said seriously.

Homicide and Artie struggled to hold back their laughter. They never thought that gangster Vega was scared of anything.

Suddenly the front door swung open and Junie and Butcher rushed into the house.

"Vega, we got us a major problem!" Butcher said.

"What is it?" Vega asked calmly.

"Carlos Benitez is dead!" Butcher said, pacing.

"What!"

"Yeah, he and two of his top men were gunned down inside a restaurant in North Philly this morning!"

Vega stood from the sofa with a concerned look on his face. He couldn't believe what he had just heard. His major drug connect was dead. Carlos was the only person Vega had ever done business with. There was no one else in the drug game he could trust.

"SHIT!" Vega yelled.

"Yeah, it's all on the radio, man! Somebody smokes him and his two boys and got away without a trace!" Butcher said. "What the hell are we gonna do now? We got nineteen drug houses that need to be up and running or we're gonna lose 'em to the competitors."

"Calm down, Butcher!" Vega shouted. "Don't worry. I want you to shut down all the drug houses until we can get a new connect. Ain't no use crying over spilled milk. We'll just lie low for a while. We have bigger things to worry about for now."

Vega was doing his best to keep his composure. But deep down inside he knew he had just received a major blow to his drug organization. With no drugs to sell, his lucrative street business would soon start to crumble. After pacing for a minute, Vega stopped and said, "We need to kill Underworld and his crew! Once they are dead, I'll find us another drug connect and this city will belong to us!"

Then he walked away, leaving behind a very worried crew.

CHAPTER 13

Underworld Entertainment

CASSIE STOOD FROM HER DESK and walked over to the window. She stared out at the beautiful blue and white August sky, watching as the birds flew through the air without a care in the world.

Riley walked up to her office door and saw her standing there looking out the window. Without disturbing her peaceful mood, he turned around and walked away. Being the president of Underworld Entertainment wasn't the easiest job in the world. The job came with a lot of ups and downs, and more ass kissing than one could ever imagine. Everyone wanted to be a star, and Cassie was in a powerful position to make a lot of people's dreams a reality.

For Cassie, there was no better joy in the world than taking a talented person from the streets and helping turn that person into a mega star. That was why she idolized people like Mary J. Blige, Keyshia Cole, Diana Ross, Fantasia, Eve, Jay-Z, Snoop Dogg, Russell Simmons, and so many others who had come from nothing and turned their lives into something very special. Even with all the daily headaches from the music producers, video directors, songwriters, wannabe divas, and spoiled, immature rappers, Cassie still wouldn't trade her job for anything in the world.

The sound of her ringing cell phone interrupted her thoughts. Cassie turned from the window and sat back down in her chair. When she looked at the caller ID to see who was calling, a big smile lit her face.

"Yes, my love, what is it?" she asked.

"Can you get away for a while?" Frank asked.

"Anything for you, my love."

"OK, good. Tell Riley to hold down the fort until tomorrow morning."

"Tomorrow morning!" Cassie said, surprised.

"Yeah. Just jump in your car and meet me at our private hanger at the airport. I'll be inside the G-4 waiting."

Cassie held the cell phone to her ear while walking out of her office.

"OK, Mister Spontaneous, where are you taking me now?" she asked as she approached Riley's office door.

"Vegas. I got us a private suite already booked at the Bellagio," Frank said.

"What's the special occasion?"

"You, and plus I need to get away and clear my mind."

"So you decided to go to Vegas to do it?"

"Why not? Remember Cancun, Jamaica, and Rio? You didn't complain about any of those trips," Frank teased.

"Who said I was complaining? I'll see you at the airport in about forty-five minutes. Make sure the pilot has our favorite red wine."

"You're late. It's already waiting for you."

"OK, my love, let me get myself together and I'm on my way. Love you."

After Cassie told Riley to take care of everything while she was gone, she rushed into the empty elevator. When she reached her brand new Jaguar XX, she got in, started it, and quickly drove out of the parking garage. With a big smile on her face, she headed straight for the airport.

Philadelphia International Airport

Sitting in a comfortable leather chair inside the company leased G-4 jet, Frank had his legs propped up enjoying the melodic, soulful voice of Musiq Soulchild. After leaving Craig and driving back home, Frank had a long talk with himself, letting tears of grief and sorrow escape through his soul and out of his eyes. The loss of his parents was hard on him, but he knew that even though it had only been a few days since their tragic death, it was now time to heal and move on. That was why he called Craig and Graveyard and told them that he was gonna call Cassie and get away. After he explained why, they both understood. Even if it was only for a day, Frank wanted to get far away from Philadelphia and go somewhere special with the woman of his life. For Frank there was no better feeling in the world than being alone with the woman he loved.

Holy Tabernacle Baptist Church

Deacon Harris was a scared man. Since the murders of Reverend Simms and his wife, he had been a nervous wreck. For fifty thousand dollars he had set up both of them to be killed. Now he regretted ever doing such a thing. But once he had taken Vega's money, there was no turning back. He and the reverend weren't seeing eye to eye on a lot of issues concerning the church, but his main motives for setting up the reverend and his wife were greed and jealously.

The reverend had a new Cadillac, while Deacon Harris and his wife drove around in his old, brown Chevy. The Simmses lived in a beautiful house in the Overbrook section of the city while Deacon Harris and his wife lived in a two-bedroom apartment they rented from the Simmses. No one had known that Deacon

Harris was a bitter, jealous man, waiting for the first opportunity to change his miserable life.
Deacon Harris became Vega's pawn, and now Deacon Harris was scared. Something deep inside his soul was sending him a haunting message. Deacon Harris had betrayed the church, his religion, and God himself. If he could rewind time and change everything back to the way it was, he would do so in a heartbeat. But he couldn't. Two people were now dead because of his greed and jealousy. As he sat at his desk, looking down at the .38 pistol he held in his trembling hand, tears ran down his terrified face.

South Street

J-Dawg sat comfortably inside one of Underworld Entertainment's company owned limousines, listening to his iPod. Two of his Brooklyn homeboys sat across from him playing the Xbox. J-Dawg removed the small headphones from his ears and laid the iPod on the seat.
"Reek, Trey, turn off the game for a minute," J-Dawg said.
Reek, a tall, dark-skinned man, reached over and pressed the button that paused the game.
"What's up, J-Dawg?" Trey asked. Trey was a short, dark-skinned man with big lips and bucked teeth.
"Yo, son, tonight we gonna visit a few of these Philly clubs," J-Dawg said.
"On a Wednesday?" Reek asked.
"Yeah, man, Philly is just like New York. They got clubs open every night of the week."
"I don't know, J-Dawg," Trey said. "Remember the last time we tried to party in one of those Philly clubs? We got into that big fight with security and you ended up catching a gun charge."

"Plus Cassie already warned you not to go to any clubs before your show next week," Reek said.

"Look here, man, Cassie don't tell me what to do," J-Dawg said. "I'm my own man. Plus I'm the one paying their bills over at Underworld Entertainment. I'm tired of staying all cooped up inside a hotel room, playing video games and watching DVDs all day. I need some excitement in my life, and a few of these Philly chicks will fill that void," J-Dawg said as they all started laughing and giving each other high fives.

"What about the gat?" Reck asked.

J-Dawg lifted up his T-shirt and pulled out a brand new black 9 mm. "I'm no fool. This time it's staying inside the limo. Tonight we gonna show the City of Brotherly Love just how we Brooklyn niggas get down."

One block away from the Philadelphia Franklin Institute, Graveyard sat on one of the outside benches waiting. Moments later, a black van pulled up and parked in front of him. A short, chubby white man got out of the van, and then got into a tan Nissan Maxima and drove off. Graveyard stood. No one outside was paying him any mind when he walked over, got inside the van, and pulled off down the street. Inside the back of the van was rope, silver duct tape, a box of new 9 mm guns, a box of police issued handcuffs, and a box of U.S. Army issued hand grenades. Craig had put in a special order for the grenades.

Graveyard was headed for Frank's private warehouse in Yeadon. Craig had already set up all the arrangements with the local police. When Graveyard reached over and opened the glove compartment, stacks of fifty- and one-hundred-dollar bills were piled inside. The money was payment for the Yeadon police officers and the three cemetery workers.

***

Over twelve thousand feet in the air Cassie could feel the powerful orgasm sweeping through her trembling body. Frank had her standing behind the leather seat with her Dolce & Gabbana dress pulled up and her Victoria's Secret thongs pulled down to her ankles. As Frank made love to her from behind, Cassie filled the air with soft, light moans. In the privacy of the jet, somewhere between earth and heaven, Frank and Cassie were both in a world of pure bliss.

The Dollhouse Gentlemen's Club

"We need to do something, Homicide!" Butcher said.

"Do what, Butcher? All we can do is wait until the boss gets us a new drug connect," Homicide said as he walked around the club, putting the chairs up on the tables.

"That can take forever! In the meantime who's gonna supply our drug houses with more product?"

"Look, Butcher, I feel your pain. Believe me I do. I'm missing a lot of money just like you, but there's nothing that either of us can do until Vega finds us another drug supplier. The only other people that got the kinda weight we wanna buy are Underworld's people. And they would kill us on the spot if they saw us."

"Damn!" Butcher said. He knew that Homicide's words were true.

"Look at the bright side, Butcher. Once Underworld is gone, we'll be the ones running this city. That's why it's important for us to stay focused and stick to the plan that Vega laid out. You know that once the head is chopped off, the rest of the body will crumble. After

Underworld is out of the way, there will be no one stopping us."

"Do you think Underworld had anything to do with Carlos and his men being killed?" Butcher asked.

"Man, you're giving Underworld too much credit. He's not in the streets no more. He's into that music company he owns. The man is probably running around with bodyguards scared for his life. He knows he's next on Vega's list. And besides, how would he know who Vega gets his drugs from if he's sitting behind a desk all day signing rappers' checks?" Homicide asked and they both started laughing. "This man is through!" Homicide continued. "He's a weak has-been. If I ever ran into him, I would kill 'im with my bare hands. I hope I see him at the rap concert next week. I would love to be the man who kills Underworld."

"You know Vega promised a hundred fifty grand for the person responsible for killing him," Butcher said.

"I know. And a hundred grand for Craig and Cassie," Homicide replied.

Butcher thought about everything that Homicide had said about Frank and realized that it all had to be true. Underworld was no longer in the streets. He had people running the streets for him while he sat back enjoying all the profits. Underworld was just living off of his once violent kingpin reputation. But neither him nor Vega was fooled. They were determined to be the two men responsible for touching the so-called Mr. Untouchable.

After Butcher left the club, he got into his Lexus and took out his cell phone. He called all his men one by one and told them to shut down all his drug houses.

Robert Steiner sat at his desk lost in the wonderful memory of his night with DNA. Last night he and his wife Emily had enjoyed the best sexual experience of their lives. The three women had turned Robert and Emily completely out. In the privacy of their bedroom, they did everything in the book of sexual pleasure. Robert Steiner and his wealthy wife Emily were two old freaks.

As Robert sat at his desk, thinking about the night before, he received another fax containing more information about Vega Littles. In just three days his file on Vega was halfway full. Robert knew that Vega Littles had crossed the wrong man.

"No one crosses Frank „Underworld' Simms and lives to tell about it," Frank once told Robert. The words never left Robert's mind. Frank Simms was more powerful than most of Robert's political friends. There was no one that Frank couldn't touch, and Robert understood this, as did so many others.

Artie could feel in his soul that something about Carlos Benitez being murdered wasn't right. He knew that it was no coincidence that Vega's only drug supplier had been suddenly shot and murdered inside a restaurant filled with people, and not one witness saw what happened. Everything about it just didn't add up. He was nobody's fool. Something kept telling him that Underworld was responsible for the hit on Carlos. But Artie knew that there would never be any proof.

Artie sat inside his car thinking about the one-hundred-fifty-thousand-dollar contract that Vega had put out on Underworld's head. He knew that Underworld would soon find out about Artie being the crooked cop on Vega's payroll. Looking over his shoulder for the rest of his life wasn't something that Artie could live with. That was why Frank "Underworld" Simms had to die. Because Artie knew that as long as Frank was still alive, a lot of men would be living in total fear.

When Artie pulled off down the street in his unmarked police car, an evil grin spread across his face. He felt that this game of cat and mouse was about to come to an end. And Underworld, Craig, and Cassie would all be joining Frank's parents in a six-foot grave.

Later that night

Graveyard stood back to watch the three cemetery workers dig out three large holes in the ground. Graveyard had found the perfect spot at the far end of an old cemetery located on Lehigh Avenue in North Philly. For two days the workers had been digging out three ten-foot graves. After the workers finished digging, Graveyard left the cemetery and headed back to his room at the Marriott. He needed to get cleaned up and ready for another late night sexcapade with Passion.

The Bellagio Hotel and Casino, Las Vegas

Inside their private luxury suite, Frank and Cassie had just finished another round of intense lovemaking. Their weekend trips to Atlantic City couldn't compare to just a few hours in the city known around the world as Sin City. Along with Miami and New York, Vegas was a non-stop celebrity party. Before retiring to their suite, Frank had lost a few grand at the crap table, and Cassie lost about the same amount at the blackjack table and the slot machines.

As the two lovers lay cuddled in each other's arms, once again they started passionately kissing. Then Cassie smiled, laid Frank back, and climbed on top of him. She started licking and sucking all around his neck. Cassie knew where every one of his sensitive spots were, and she made sure her warm, wet tongue touched them all.

Cassie grabbed her thongs from the floor and tied them tightly around Frank's wrists. She then lifted his arms above his head and said, "Don't say a word."

Frank watched as Cassie reached across the bed and grabbed one of the silk sheets. He lay there watching as she tied the sheet around his ankles. When she was finished, Cassie climbed back on top of her handsome, naked, prey and said, "This is some get back for what you did to me on that jet!"

Then in one smooth motion, Cassie slid Frank's thick, hard dick into the deepness of her inviting love cave. While Frank's tied up body lay there, Cassie started riding him like a veteran porn star, matching him stroke for stroke, thrust for thrust. In the privacy of their suite, Cassie gave Frank a sex lesson to remember.

Chapter 14

Thursday afternoon

"WHAT THE HELL IS GOING on?" Agent Stokes asked as he sat inside the white Ford van, looking out the tinted windows.

"Beats me," his partner Mitchell said.

For two long hours they had been posted down the street from Butcher's drug house on Thirty-ninth Street. But unlike all the other days they had watched the street, today there was no traffic coming or going. Crackheads and dopefiends were walking right past the house.

"Maybe they ran out of drugs," Stokes said.

"Yeah, right. Butcher is one of the biggest drug dealers around. If anyone has drugs, it's him. And once we have one of his houses raided and confiscate some guns and drugs, we're gonna bring him down, then use him to get us Vega."

"Let's go check out his other drug houses," Stokes said, starting up the van and pulling off.

After driving a few blocks, they parked the van on the corner of Forty-first and Poplar streets. And just like the Thirty-ninth Street drug house, there was no traffic coming or going. Stokes started up the van and drove a few more blocks until he reached the corner of Forty-ninth and Hope streets. This was a well known drug area that was also controlled by some of Butcher's men. Nothing. Not a single fiend was in sight.

"What in the hell is going on!" Mitchell yelled.
"What is it, National Don't-Get-High-Off-Crack Day!"
"Something surely ain't right," Stokes said. "Butcher hasn't been around all day, and all of his drug houses are closed down. Besides that, we can't even get close to Frank and his Underworld crew. This investigation is really starting to piss me off!"

"We've been posted outside Underworld Entertainment all week, and have only seen Frank and his partner Craig once. And all we got on Vega so far is some bullshit surveillance notes of him coming and going to his club," Mitchell said, slamming his fist down on the dashboard. "Come on, let's get the hell out of here."

"Where to next?" Stokes asked.

"Let's go get something to eat, and then we can swing back by Underworld Entertainment. Maybe we'll get lucky and spot Frank," Mitchell said.

With a disappointed look on his face, Stokes started the van and pulled off.

Downtown Philadelphia

Robert Steiner had helped Frank put together an airtight company. Underworld Entertainment was its own unique entity, complete with staff and board members. Underworld Entertainment also owned many non-profit corporations that held titles to property throughout Philadelphia, and in other major cities along the East Coast. Frank had made sure that nothing was in his name, knowing that the only way the feds liked to play was dirty. They would come in and take away everything a person owned, then sell it at one of their government auctions. Or they would forfeit people's assets and freeze every bank account they owned. That was why Frank made sure that every one of his homes and cars were all owned by Underworld Entertainment.

Robert Steiner got off the elevator and walked through the plush lobby of his law firm. When he walked through the large glass doors, holding a black briefcase in his hand, he patiently waited. The sidewalks were crowed with people. He thought about running over and grabbing a chili dog, but the outside vendor had a line almost a half block long. The sun was beaming hard, but the tall downtown skyscrapers provided lots of shade.

Robert stood there watching the cars, cabs, and bikes drive up and down the congested streets. Suddenly a black tinted limousine pulled up in front of the building and double parked. Robert quickly ran over to the limo and got inside. Then the limo slowly pulled off down the street. Inside the spacious limousine, Frank and Craig were sitting next to each other, discussing some important business.

"Frank, Craig, it's good to see y'all again," Robert said as he shook both men's hands.

Robert sat back and got himself more comfortable. Then he set the briefcase he was holding on his lap and popped it open. He reached inside, grabbed a large brown envelope, and passed it over to Frank.

"That's everything on your boy, Vega," Robert said. "You'll see when you check it out." He smiled. Frank nodded and set down the envelope. Then Craig pulled out a large stack of hundreds and tossed them over to Robert. Robert caught the stack of money in mid air.

"That's the other twenty-five thousand I promised you," Frank said.

"Thank you, Frank. So how was your trip to Vegas last night?" he asked.

"Wonderful, and very therapeutic," Frank said, cracking a smile. "Me and Cassie got back early this morning."

"Well it's always good to see you in high spirits, especially with all that's been going on. Our friend Peter down at the DA's office supplied me with a lot of useful information."

"I already know. Peter told me two days ago," Frank said.

"I should've known," Robert replied. "Frank, if there's anything else you need, remember I'm always just a call away," Robert said, putting the money inside his briefcase and closing it.

"I know, Robert. That's why I love you, my good friend," Frank said, tapping him on the leg.

When the limo stopped, Robert looked out the window and saw that he was back at his office building. He opened the door, then paused.

"Frank, umm . . ."

"DNA will be by your house later. Have a good day, Robert," Frank said.

When Robert got out and closed the door, Frank and Craig both busted out in laughter.

Southwest Philly

Junie drove the white Cadillac Escalade while Vega sat in the passenger seat. Homicide was inside a brown Jeep Cherokee, following right behind them. When the trucks pulled up and parked in front of the house, they all exited the vehicles. Homicide got out of the Jeep carrying two large Neiman Marcus shopping bags and another bag from City Blue. They entered the house where Butcher, Artie, Spade, and Canon were already waiting.

"Jewell, Cindy, come down here," Vega shouted upstairs.

Dressed in all black Victoria's Secret lingerie, both girls rushed downstairs.

"Here," Vega said, taking one of the Neiman Marcus bags from Homicide and passing it to Cindy. "That's for y'all," he said.

With big smiles on their faces, both girls rushed back upstairs.

"Homicide, give 'em their stuff," Vega said as he sat down in the empty love seat. Homicide reached into the larger City Blue bag and pulled out six red Phillies baseball caps. After he passed them all out he placed the last cap on his own head. Homicide then went into the bag and pulled out six red and white Phillies baseball jerseys. Once again he passed one to everyone inside the room.

"I figured y'all might as well have the jerseys to go with them," Vega said. "Go get the walkie-talkies," Vega told Junie.

Junie walked out the room.

"What's in the other bags?" Butcher asked.

"Oh, a few things I bought for Raquel and Erika."

When Junie came back into the room, he was carrying six new high-powered walkie-talkies. He passed them around.

"I'll have all the new guns by Monday," Vega said.

Spade and Canon both beamed with excitement. They had been yearning for a kill for days.

"Where's that damn snake, Spade?" Vega asked when he noticed her smile.

"I left Hulk at home," she answered with a grin on her face.

"Make sure you keep his ugly green ass at home," Vega said as he stood. "OK, everybody, I'll call y'all when I need y'all again. Oh, by the way, I've changed the contract that I put on Underworld's head."

"What is it now?" Butcher asked.

"Two hundred thousand cash for whoever kills him. And one hundred fifty for Craig and Cassie," Vega said. "May the best killer succeed." Vega laughed.

After Junie let everyone out of the house, Vega walked upstairs to his beautiful mistresses. Junie sat on the sofa with an evil smirk on his face. *Underworld, Craig, and Cassie, come next week, y'all will be three dead motherfuckers. And I'll be a whole lot richer,* he thought.

Chapter 15

Underworld Entertainment

"Cassie, Cassie, Cassie," a female voice called out.

Cassie quickly lifted her head from her desk and realized that she had dozed off. Valerie, her tall, attractive brown-skinned secretary was calling her name.

"What is it, Val?"

"Cassie, J-Dawg got into some trouble," Val said.

"What is it now? And where the hell is he?" Cassie asked.

"He's in jail."

"Jail?" Cassie snapped as she stood from her chair. "What the hell happened this time?"

"J-Dawg was involved in a fight at one of those clubs down Delaware Avenue last night. He just got his phone call about fifteen minutes ago. He told me what happened."

"What did he say?" Cassie asked, sitting back down in her chair.

"He said that some jealous guy who was there at the club tried to snatch his necklace and run. J-Dawg caught the guy and they got into a fistfight. The cops arrested both of them."

"What's wrong with that boy? I've told him time after time about hanging in those thugged-out Philly clubs. Did the cops find a weapon on him this time?"

"No. Just his cell phone and a few thousand dollars in his pockets."

Cassie sat there shaking her head in disgust.

"What's wrong with these new rappers? I'm really getting tired of J-Dawg's shit! That boy knows he has a show to perform next week at the Civic Center."

"Do you want me to tell Riley to go down to the police station and pick him up?"

"No. J-Dawg needs to be taught a valuable lesson this time. Don't worry, I know exactly how to handle it. I'm glad you came by, Val. I wanted to talk with you anyway."

"Yes, Cassie, what's up?" Val asked as she approached Cassie's desk.

"How are all the new interns turning out?"

"So far so good. Riley and I stay on them and make sure they are on their jobs. They're all sitting at their cubicles now," Val said, pointing her finger out the door.

"Good." Cassie smiled.

"You sure you don't want me to tell Riley to go get J-Dawg?"

"I'm positive. Don't worry, somebody will pick him up," Cassie said with a smile.

After Valerie left the office, Cassie grabbed her cell phone and made a quick call. When she hung up the phone she sat back with an even bigger smile on her face. After a long sigh, Cassie stared into her computer screen, then once again started attacking her keyboard.

"Do you believe this, Stokes?" Agent Mitchell asked. "Every one of Butcher's drug houses is shut down! And Frank never shows up at his own company! This investigation is starting off real fucked up!"

"Well maybe we'll have some better luck tomorrow," Stokes said as he started up the van and drove down Thirty-fifth Street.

"Let's just hope so, because at the rate this investigation is going, when we do finally get some indictments, Frank, Craig, Vega, and Butcher will all be senior citizens," Mitchell said.

Thirtieth and Girard

Sitting inside the limousine, Frank and Craig were going through all the information that Robert had gathered on Vega Littles. Graveyard was seated right across from them. Robert had managed to come up with more info on Vega than Frank expected. In Frank's hand were written documents on Vega Littles's whole life—his Social Security number, a photocopy of his driver's license, a listing of all the property he owned, his wife's full name, his only daughter's full name, and so much more vital information. There was even some info on Vega's dead, adoptive parents. Altogether, Frank had every piece of information he needed on Vega.

They all perused each piece of paper. When they were done Frank looked over at Graveyard and said, "I'll get you a crew of my best men to help you take care of everything. Just save Vega for me."

"I'll start preparing things now. But first I have to check out these spots. I should be ready in a few days," Graveyard said.

"Take your time. I just want everything done perfectly," Frank said.

On the opposite side of town

Deacon Harris was seated inside his church office, staring out at nothing. All day long he had been a nervous wreck. His conscience had been eating him alive.

An older, heavyset woman tapped on the door and walked inside the office.

"Deacon, deacon," she said.

Deacon Harris nervously jumped from his seat like a man possessed.

"What! What! What is it!" he asked, looking around his empty office.

"I'm sorry to disturb you, sir, but the choir wanted you to hear the new song they're singing for the Simmses' funeral tomorrow," the lady said.

"I'm sorry, Sister Mathis. I'll be right out there in one moment," Deacon Harris said as he stood from his desk.

"Deacon, are you OK? You've been acting a little strange lately. I've been meaning to have a talk with you," Sister Mathis said.

"I'm fine. I'll be OK. I just have a lot on my mind. That's all."

Sister Mathis looked deep into Deacon Harris's eyes and said, "We're all hurt and devastated by what happened to the reverend and his wife. Lord knows how much I cried all this week. They were two good, God fearing Christians who didn't deserve to die the way they did. But the Lord will punish everyone who is responsible for their deaths. Proverbs 14:19 says, „The evil bow before the good; and the wicked at the gates of the righteous.' And Proverbs 17:11 states, „An evil man seeks only rebellion: therefore a cruel messenger shall be sent against him.'"

Deacon Harris just stood there shaking his head.

"So don't worry, Deacon," Sister Mathis continued. "Whoever murdered the Simmses will get what's coming," she said before turning and walking away.

Later that night

After a long day of dealing with lawyers, judges, and paralegals, it was now time for Robert to enjoy himself.

He sat completely naked at the foot of his bed and watched as the three black women turned his wife's ass completely out. While Emily and one of the women were locked in a long, passionate kiss, the other two women had dildos inside Emily's asshole and pussy. Robert sat there masturbating while watching the best X-rated show of his life. Even though Frank would always take care of everything, Robert still gave the girls a nice hefty tip before they left.

After the girls left Emily drained of all her sexual energy, they looked over at Robert.

"OK, big boy, it's your turn," one of the girls said.

Center City Philadelphia

J-Dawg walked out of the downtown police station and saw the black limousine parked outside waiting on him. He eagerly rushed over and quickly got inside. When he climbed inside he was very surprised to see Frank sitting there. Craig was also inside the limo, sitting next to Graveyard. J-Dawg had heard all about Frank's violent street reputation. On the street, Frank "Underworld" Simms's name was legendary. J-Dawg tried his best to make himself comfortable.

"Hey, Mr. Simms," he said in a timid voice.

Frank didn't say a word. He just sat there with a serious look on his face.

After thirty minutes of driving, the limousine stopped in a dark, secluded area in Fairmount Park.

"Get out," Frank said.

"Huh?" J-Dawg asked.

"Get the fuck out now!" Frank yelled.

J-Dawg quickly grabbed the door handle and stepped outside. When he looked around there was nothing but grass and tall trees. Frank, Craig, and Graveyard all stepped out of the limo. J-Dawg was terrified.

"Please, man, don't kill me!" he pleaded.

"Shut the fuck up, you little punk!" Frank said.

Graveyard pulled out a chrome .40-caliber gun and pointed it at J-Dawg's head.

"So you think you're a real gangster, huh?" Frank asked.

"Please, Mr. Simms, please!" J-Dawg said as the tears started rolling down his face.

"Go and stand over by the car, you little punk! If you try to run, I swear my man will put a bullet in the back of your brain!"

J-Dawg walked over to the limo and stood beside it.

"Turn around and put your hands on the hood, punk! But first slide down your jeans and underwear."

"Huh?"

"You heard me. Now don't make me tell you again!" Frank ordered.

J-Dawg did as he was told and slid down his jeans and underwear. He stood there with his bare ass sticking out, wondering what the hell he had gotten himself into. In one smooth motion Frank slid his thick, leather belt from around his waist. After he wrapped it tightly around his fist, he walked up behind J-Dawg and said, "You better not move, you little punk!"

Frank raised his arm high in the air, then brought it back down like a bolt of lighting. *Smack!*

"AHH!" J-Dawg yelled.
"Shut up you little ass punk and take it like a man!"
Smack! Smack! Smack!
Craig and Graveyard stood there watching as Frank whipped J-Dawg's ass. Literally. Every time Frank slammed the leather belt against his ass, J-Dawg screamed like a man on the brink of death.
Smack! Smack! Smack!
After five whole minutes of slamming the thick leather belt against J-Dawg's bare ass, Frank finally stopped. J-Dawg's bruised ass had turned two shades darker.
"Now pull up your pants and turn around," Frank said.
J-Dawg tearfully did as he was told. Frank reached out and grabbed his shirt collar.
"Look here, you fake ass gangster, all the real fucking gangsters are dead or serving football numbers in prison. And a lot more are serving life! You're a motherfucking rapper! I don't give a fuck how many people you kill on your records. This is the real world, not some fake wannabe gangster who kills and commits crimes on the mic! When my company signed you, you were nothing but a broke ass little punk! Underworld Entertainment made you an instant millionaire and helped get your poor ass family out of Brooklyn and into a nice home in Jersey. This shit is not a game! And you need to start treating this business that saved you with a little more respect! In four years won't nobody remember you, you dumb motherfucker! There will be a new young rapper taking your place. I'ma give you the best advice I can. Get all the money in this industry you can get now, and get out before you get thrown out or taken out! If you keep fucking up, J-Dawg, and I have to come for you again, the next time will be your

last. I better not never hear a bad word about you again. You hear me!" Frank yelled.
"Yes! Yes, Mr. Simms, I . . . hear you," J-Dawg mumbled.
"Now get your black ass in the limo so I can have you dropped off at your hotel."
J-Dawg hurried into the limo. When he sat down his ass started burning. For the young, wannabe gangster, it was the first beating he'd ever received in his entire life.
Graveyard put his gun back under his shirt and climbed into the limo. J-Dawg never looked his way. Instead he kept his head to the floor the whole ride, Realizing that he wasn't the gangster that he thought he was. And tonight J-Dawg had learned a valuable lesson, one that would stay with him for the rest of his life—all the real gangsters were dead or in prison.

City Line Avenue

Inside his well furnished living room, Vega lay across the soft, leather sectional with his pregnant wife Raquel wrapped inside his arms. Just a few feet away Erika also lay on the couch. They were all laughing and enjoying Eddie Murphy's *The Nutty Professor*. A half eaten pizza lay on top of the coffee table.
Vega loved his family more than anything in the world, and he spoiled them with everything his money could buy. He also kept them as far away from his illegal street activities as possible. Vega understood the heartless drug game as well as anyone. He knew that a person's enemy's first target was always that person's loved ones. That was why no one knew where he and his family rested their heads except for Junie.
Vega knew how a person could be a friend one day, and an enemy the next, so he didn't trust anybody. The

drug game was the most vicious game that existed. Brothers killed their own brothers. And even kids murdered their own parents. Vega knew this. He had been living this violent life for too many years. He lost his brother Tony because of it, and now he was determined to reverse his brother's death by killing the man who was responsible.

After the movie ended, Vega watched as Raquel and Erika walked upstairs to get ready for bed. Vega turned out all the lights downstairs, and then followed his family upstairs. He headed straight back to his small, private room. He stepped inside the room, closed the door, and retrieved a large brown box from the closet.

After sitting down in his chair, he opened the box. Inside were a few baby pictures—pictures of him, Tony, and their deceased parents—plus a few other personal items. Vega reached past everything and took out three white pieces of paper. One of them was a duplicate copy of his birth certificate. The other two pieces of paper were even more personal. Vega sat back in his chair and stared at all three papers. In the quietness of his room, a lonely tear escaped from the corner of his left eye. After a long sigh, Vega stood and put the box back inside the closet. He placed the box on a top shelf, then closed the door.

Since the day Vega had put out the contract on Frank's parents, his mind had been clouded with disturbing thoughts. He couldn't wait for the day when Frank would join his dead parents. Frank was the only man who stood in his way of controlling the Philadelphia drug trade, and Vega would not rest until his number one nemesis was buried inside a grave beside his two dead parents.

CHAPTER 16

Friday afternoon

OUTSIDE THE HOLY TABERNACLE BAPTIST Church, a few of Frank's men stood around watching for anything that looked or seemed out of place. Tucked inside their black suit jackets were loaded 9 mm pistols. Frank wasn't taking any unnecessary chances. His parents had already been savagely gunned down outside the church, so he was making sure that no one else he loved would meet the same fate.

Inside the crowded house of God, people were sitting around crying and calling on the Lord. The two all-white caskets surrounded by dozens of beautiful, colorful flowers sat in front of the large podium. Both bodies were dressed in all white.

While the choir members sang the original song they had written and dedicated to the Simmses, Frank couldn't help but keep his focus on Deacon Harris. The deacon had seemed nervous and uncomfortable the whole morning. And Frank could sense that there was something eating him up inside. Every time Deacon Harris looked over at Frank, Frank could feel his demons pulling and yanking at his grieving soul.

Cassie sat on the right side of Frank, holding his hand. When she looked into his eyes, there were no tears, no looks of sadness, pain, misery, or grief. Frank knew that both of his loving parents were now in a much better place. On Frank's left side sat his younger cousin, Tadpole, and his best friend, Craig—two men that Frank trusted with his life. When Frank looked around for Graveyard, he spotted him walking through the door. He knew that Graveyard was a very serious person when it came to security. Graveyard was a watcher by nature, a man that always made sure his surroundings were safe.

After the funeral ended and everyone viewed the bodies for the final time, they all started walking out of the church.

Two all white Mercedes Benz stretch limousines were parked in front of the church. Frank, Cassie, Tadpole, and Craig all got inside one while a few other close family members got inside the other limo. After both caskets were placed inside an all white hearse, the cars pulled off. The sun was shining brightly and the sky was a brilliant blue with fluffy white clouds. Frank looked out the window, up toward heaven. For a few moments he just stared out into the calm sky. Peace entered his soul.

Frank turned and looked at Cassie and Craig. With a big smile on his face, he said, "God has 'em now. They're all right. After the burial, instead of being sad, let's get out of town for a night and go celebrate."

"Are you sure, baby?" Cassie asked.

"I'm positive!"

Outside the church

Two pairs of blue eyes watched everything from inside an unmarked car. Agents Mitchell and Stokes had finally gotten another chance to see Frank "Underworld" Simms and his partner in crime, Craig Morris.

"So they are still alive," Mitchell joked.

"Yeah, and neither of them looked too happy," Stokes said.

"Hell, I wouldn't be happy either if I just saw both of my parents laid out in caskets beside each other. Don't these people ever get tired of killing their own?"

"I guess not, because if they did, the murder rate in the black community wouldn't be so damn high," Stokes said.

"Well let 'em continue to sell drugs and kill each other off. That way I'll always have a job," Mitchell said and laughed.

After all the cars had pulled off down the street, Agent Stokes started up the car and drove off.

On the opposite side of the street, Officer Artie Fletcher was inside his car scoping out the area. Tucked inside his blue jeans was a black 9 mm Beretta, fully loaded and ready to kill Frank Simms on sight. But unfortunately for Artie, he never got a good look at his victim. There were too many people standing around for him to get off a clear shot. Plus Artie had noticed the five large black men dressed in all black that were posted all around the front of the church. He was positive that they were Frank's men. And at the first sign of danger, none of them would hesitate to pull out their licensed weapons and start shooting. Artie knew that it would be a no-win situation, and his carelessness and impatience would only cost him his own life. *There will be another time and another place,* he thought. After starting up his car, he slowly drove off in the opposite direction of the funeral procession.

Standing on the roof of the church, Graveyard watched everything from high above. He had gotten the keys to the roof from Deacon Harris an hour before anyone had arrived at the church. Graveyard noticed that the two agents were the same two he had seen before. Through his binoculars he watched as they sat inside their unmarked police car.

Graveyard smiled, knowing that the two agents were way over their heads. It was just a matter of time before their snooping would all come to an end. But what confused Graveyard was the other unmarked police car with one black man sitting inside. Graveyard knew the man was a cop. He could smell a cop a mile away. Looking through his binoculars, he made sure he got a good look at the cop's face. He knew that he would be seeing that man around again, and something deep down inside his gut was telling him that the next time he saw the man, it wouldn't be a pretty sight.

Southwest Philly

"A lot of people showed up at the Simmses' funeral. Cars were lined up all down the street," Artie said.

Pacing with a big smile on his face, Vega said, "Did you get to see Underworld?"

"No, there were too many people around. Plus Underworld had his security team posted all around the church. I did see the two white caskets, though," Artie said as he stood from the sofa.

"So Frank buried his poor mommy and daddy in all white, huh?" Vega asked. "Well soon he'll be joining them, and then they can all be the perfect little family again," Vega said as he sat back down on the sofa.

Artie looked over Vega's beaming face and shook his head in confusion. Vega was an enigma. Artie had never seen a man get so much pleasure out of seeing someone's parents get killed.

The front door opened and Vega's two lovely ladies walked inside carrying Macy's and Saks Fifth Avenue shopping bags. They closed the front door and rushed over to Vega's side. Each woman gave him a kiss on the cheek.

"Did y'all enjoy y'all's weekly shopping spree?" he asked.

"Yes, daddy, thank you so much," Jewell said.

"We bought you some new underwear," Cindy added.

"For what?" Vega laughed. "I never get a chance to wear them. Y'all can go upstairs now. I'll be up there shortly."

Vega and Artie watched as both women grabbed all their shopping bags and rushed up the stairs.

"Are you looking forward to next week's rap concert?" Vega asked.

"I can't wait. I'll be hanging around back. My badge will get me past all the security."

"Easier said than done. Frank's not stupid. He'll probably have his security team watching his back, just like he had at the funeral today."

"It won't matter. None of Frank's people know who I am," Artie said with confidence. "Vega, I'll see you in a few days. Call me if you need me," Artie said while walking over to the door.

"I sure will," Vega said as he stood from the sofa.

After Artie left, Vega locked the front door and walked up the stairs where his two young beauties were naked and waiting for him.

West Philadelphia

Inside their small bedroom, Spade and Canon faced each other while holding hands. Both were completely naked. A cloud of incense smoke filled the bedroom. Posters of Satan, angels, witches, warlocks, and demons filled the four walls. With four large candles situated

throughout the room, Hulk, their four feet long green snake slid around Spade's naked body.
No one in Vega's crew understood these two. Not even Vega, who had met the two young assassins at a traveling circus where they used to work. But Vega didn't care what the weird young couple was into. They were his two best assassins. Each of them got great pleasure from murder.
"Death is life," Canon said.
"Death is life," Spade repeated.
For a few moments they just stared deep into each other's eyes. Then they started passionately kissing.

North Philadelphia

Inside a small row house on Fifth and Cambria streets, four Dominican men sat at a table talking. One of the men was Tito Benitez, the boss of the New York, New Jersey, and Dominican drug cartel, and the father of Carlos Benitez. Tito was forty-seven-years-old with a dark brown complexion and a tall, slim frame. Four years earlier he sent his only son, Carlos, to Philly to take over his illegal drug business. Now his twenty-eight-year-old son and two of his top men were dead. And Tito was determined to get some answers.

Tito stood from the table and looked around at the three men with him. The room suddenly got quiet. A look of hurt and pain filled Tito's brown eyes. The three men all watched in silence as Tito stood there shaking his head. Finally he spoke.

"I don't care how long it takes, but I want whoever was responsible for my son's death found and brought to me!"

"Mr. Benitez, we've been on it since the day of the murders, and so far no one knows a thing," one of the men said. "Whoever was behind the hit planned it perfectly."

Bam! Tito slammed his fist down on the wooden table and yelled, "I don't care! I don't care if it takes twenty fucking years! Find out who killed my son!"

"We will, Mr. Benitez. We will," the man said nervously.

"My son's body will be buried in New York next week. Then I'm going on a short vacation with my wife and two daughters. I will return back to Philadelphia in about a month. When I return, I want some answers," Tito said.

The three men watched as Mr. Benitez grabbed his jacket. Then they all stood and followed Tito out of the room. They walked Mr. Benitez to the front door where one of his personal bodyguards stood around waiting for him. They all walked outside and saw a brand new white Mercedes Benz GL parked in front of the house. Unknown to the three men, a man sat behind the driver's seat with a loaded .45 pistol tucked underneath his T-shirt.

The three men watched as Mr. Benitez and his bodyguard got inside the Mercedes. Then they watched as the car slowly drove off, headed back to New York City. The three men looked at each other, clearly worried. They only had a month to find out some answers about the mysterious murder of Carlos Benitez.

CHAPTER 17

Later that night

DOWN IN THE BASEMENT OF the Dollhouse Gentlemen's Club, Butcher stood back laughing while Homicide beat a skinny white man to the brink of death. Butcher watched as Homicide punched, smacked, and kicked his victim to the hard, cold floor.

"Mothafucker, you better never disrespect one of my girls again!" Homicide shouted. Blood covered the man's entire face. His nose, jaw, and ribs were all broken. The man had made the biggest mistake of his life when he disrespected one the club's strippers by calling her a nigger whore.

After the stripper told Homicide what the man had called her, Homicide walked up, grabbed him by his shirt, and dragged the man down to the beat down room—the basement. Now that Homicide was done, he dragged the man up some steps that led to the back of the building. Butcher followed Homicide outside and watched as he dropped the body to the ground. Two of Butcher's goons stood around waiting for instructions.

"Drop this white trash off at the park somewhere!" Butcher said.

"Do you want him to wake up in the morning?" one of the men asked.

Butcher looked over at the beaten man and said, "Fuck 'im. Let the cops earn they money!"

Then he and Homicide both turned around and calmly walked back into the club.

Parked right out front of the club, Agents Mitchell and Stokes had no idea that a man had just been severely beaten inside the club, and that the car that was driving past them was carrying the beaten man to his final resting place.

"Come on, ain't nothing happening here tonight," Stokes said. "Same old shit. Maybe Vega will come through tomorrow." Stokes started up the car and pulled off down the street.

"Next week we're sending in one of our paid street informants," Mitchell said. "That should get his investigation moving."

Graveyard sat on the bed inside his hotel room reading over a list of all of Vega's personal properties—two small car dealerships, a soul food restaurant on Lancaster Avenue, a pool hall on Fortieth Street, a beauty salon/barbershop on Fifty-eighth Street, a home in Southwest Philly, and another home around the City Line Avenue area. All the cars and trucks that Vega owned were also on the list. And a gentlemen's social club he owned in Center City was also listed. Graveyard stood and grabbed his keys from the dresser just as Passion was walking out of the bathroom. A white silk robe covered her naked body.

"Where are you going now?" she asked.

"I gotta go check out something," Graveyard said, walking over to the door. Passion didn't say a word when Graveyard rushed out the door. Being a woman from the streets, she understood. After getting dressed, Passion left the hotel room. Sexual pleasure was good, but her lucrative street business always came first.

Los Angeles

After they shopped in the famous stores along Rodeo Drive and Robertson Boulevard, Frank had the limo driver take Cassie and him back to the mansion in the Hollywood hills. The mansion was owned by Frank's friend and major drug supplier, Juan Sanchez. The huge mansion was worth over seven million dollars. It was a beautiful, all white, tri-level home that was situated high above the Sunset Strip. The house had a twenty-foot living room ceiling, a master bedroom suite featuring a deck and a home theatre, six large bedrooms, eight bathrooms, and every other room a person could imagine inside its five thousand nine hundred square feet of space.

Inside the elegant master bedroom, Frank and Cassie lay in bed talking.

"If we keep this up, we're gonna both get fired," Cassie said as she laid her head across Frank's stomach.

"Don't you worry about that, sweetie. Me and the boss are pretty tight," Frank said.

"Does Mr. Sanchez ever be here?" she asked.

"Probably not. He has homes like this one all around the world. You should see the ones in Miami and the Hamptons."

"And he gave you complete access to all of them, huh?" Cassie asked with a smile.

"Yup. Lucky me," Frank said as he ran his fingers through her long, silky black hair. "The pilot said that the planes will be ready for us in the morning."

"Why leave so soon? We just got here. I called Riley, and he and Valerie got everything under control."

"I have a few things to take care of back in Philly tomorrow afternoon," Frank said.

Cassie sat up on the bed and looked into Frank's eyes. "Frank, tell me what your were thinking about earlier when you were staring out at the sky."

Frank sat up beside Cassie and grabbed both of her hands. "When I was staring at the sky, I could feel in my heart that my parents were in a much better place. So if a person truly believes in a place called heaven, then why sit around crying after a loved one's death? Instead we should be enjoying and celebrating their new life in heaven. I know that my parents are both there. It's the place that they prepared themselves to go to their whole lives!"

Cassie smiled. She had never thought about death in that way. That was why she loved Frank so much—not just because of his looks or wealth, but because Frank was a man who possessed a totally different outlook on life. Frank was a man unlike any she had ever met before. He was her king.

"Where's Craig?" Cassie asked, changing the subject.

"He was downstairs talking to someone on his cell phone," Frank said as they both laid their naked bodies back down on the bed.

Cassie rolled herself on top of Frank's stomach. After kissing his chest and neck, she said, "OK, now finish telling me about that ass-whipping you gave to our wannabe gangster J-Dawg."

Inside the large master bedroom, they both started laughing.

Philadelphia, PA

Graveyard sat inside his black Dodge Magnum, watching the two men who stood outside the Dollhouse Gentlemen's Club in Center City. Looking through his night vision binoculars, he saw both men and women walked in and out of the club. Most of the men inside the club were white upper class businessmen. The beautiful young women that entered the club were of all different races.

Graveyard saw a huge man walk out of the club and light up a blunt. The man calmly walked past the two security guards and over to a parked, tan-colored Toyota Camry. The man had to be at least seven feet tall. Graveyard kept the binoculars focused on the giant. He watched him lean against the car and start smoking the blunt. Graveyard was sure that the man was one of Vega's personal bodyguards. The man had the look and physique of a cold-blooded killer.

After Graveyard put away his binoculars, he backed up his car and drove off in the opposite direction. Graveyard was taught always to go for the biggest guy first. When the right moment and time presented itself, that was just what he intended to do.

Los Angeles

Craig stood in front of the large mansion watching as the black limousine pulled up and parked. He walked over and opened the back door. The gorgeous Janell Jones stepped out of the limo, looking like she had just walked off the pages of *Ocean Drive Magazine*. After removing her dark Gucci shades, they embraced in a long, passionate kiss. The limo pulled off, leaving them standing out front all alone.

"How long can you stay out?" Craig asked as he wrapped his arms around her waist.

"How long will you be in LA?" Janell asked in a soft, sexy voice.

"I'm going back to Philly in the morning."

"Fine. Then that's how long I'm gonna stay," Janell said as she kissed him gently on the lips. "I didn't expect you to call me saying that you were out here in the hills at one of your friend's mansions," Janell said as they walked into the house.

"You're not the only one who can pop up out of the blue," Craig said, holding her hand while walking toward the wide, spiral stairs.

"Wow, this is a very beautiful home," Janell said, looking around at all the beauty and elegance that the home possessed.

"Not as beautiful as you," Craig said as they reached the top of the stairs.

They watched a short, white butler dressed in all black come out of one of the rooms.

"Is there anything you need, sir?" he asked in his English accent.

"Yes, Stuart. You can bring us up some fresh strawberries and a bottle of champagne,"

Craig said as he opened the door to his private bedroom.

"Will do," the butler said, walking away.

"Strawberries and champagne, huh?" Janell asked, following Craig into the bedroom and closing the door.

"Yes, 'cause tonight my love can't wait," Craig said.

Philadelphia, PA
Inside a small apartment on Fifty-third and Locust

"Nora, come down here," Deacon Harris said.

Deacon Harris's wife walked out of the bathroom and down the stairs. Deacon Harris was sitting on the sofa with a worried look on his face. Nora quickly walked over to his side and sat down. She stared into his distant eyes. They had been married for nineteen years and had an eighteen-year-old son who was currently spending the summer with his cousins in

Norfolk, Virginia. They never had much, but they always had each other. Twenty years earlier they had met at a neighborhood block party, and had been together every day since. Nora saw the concern on her husbands face and said, "Honey, talk to me. Tell me what's wrong."
Deacon Harris just sat there shaking his head. Suddenly tears started falling down his face. "I did something terribly wrong, Nora!"
Nora reached out, grabbed his trembling hands, and said, "Whatever it is you did, honey, our God will forgive you."
Deacon Harris reached under the sofa and pulled out a brown paper bag. "Here. This is for you and our son."
"What is it?"
"It's fifty thousand dollars," he said as he stood.
"Honey, where—"
"Nora, please, no questions. Just do what you have to do with the money," he said as he walked toward the stairs.

Los Angeles

When Cassie tiptoed out of the bedroom to go down to the kitchen, Janell was walking down the hall toward her, returning back from the kitchen. The two attractive women stopped in the middle of the hallway and greeted each other. Both of them were dressed in long white robes with nothing on underneath. From all the industry parties and awards shows they attended, they had gotten to know each other well. Cassie was the only woman who knew about Janell and Craig's secret relationship.

"So Joe let you get out for a few, huh?" Cassie asked jokingly.

"Sometimes he can be such a pain in the ass," Janell replied.

"You know he only wants the best for you," Cassie said as they walked over to the banister and stared out at the beautifully furnished home.

"Craig is the best for me. I ain't never met a man like him."

"Believe me, there's just something about being with a bad boy," Cassie said as they both started giggling. "Craig is a good man. He's rich, handsome, and single. A good catch, if you ask me."

"I know, and I don't know what it is, Cassie, but I can't get that man out of my system. And to be honest, I don't ever want to," Janell said in a serious voice.

"All I can say, Janell, is follow your heart. Don't let someone else make the mistake for you that you would never have made for yourself. A lot of people are lonely and miserable. Don't let their disease affect you," Cassie said, putting her arm around Janell's shoulder.

For the next half hour the two women stood in the hallway talking. They found out that they both had a lot in common. They were two successful, ambitious, persistent beautiful black women who were both deeply in love with a bad boy.

CHAPTER 18

Saturday morning

DEACON HARRIS WAS ALONE INSIDE the church. At least he thought he was. Back inside the small office that used to belong to Reverend Simms, Deacon Harris sat at the desk sipping a hot cup of tea. It was a habit for him to come to the church early every morning. The funeral and burial had taken their toll on him. Not once did he look at either of the corpses. Inside his grieving heart he knew that he was to blame for the Simmses' tragic deaths.

Deacon Harris heard footsteps and he quickly jumped up from his seat. The .38 pistol he owned was inside the top drawer. He nervously walked over to the office door and opened it. Walking down the hall toward him were two young adults. A fake smile came to his face as he asked, "How can I help y'all?"

"By dying!" Spade said as she and Canon quickly pulled out 9 mm pistols and aimed them at the deacon's head. Before the deacon could run or scream out for any help, five bullets penetrated his body—two in his head and three in his chest. Spade and Canon watched as the deacon's lifeless body slumped hard to the wooden floor. Then Spade stood over his dead body and shot him three more times in the head.

The two assassins placed their weapons back inside their jackets and calmly walked away. After walking outside, they rushed around the corner and got into a waiting blue Range Rover.

As soon as they closed the doors, Junie quickly pulled off down the street. Ten minutes later Junie pulled up at the corner of Fifty-second and Market streets. Spade and Canon both got out of the SUV. Junie watched as they walked up the stairs to catch the train, and then he drove away.

Back inside the church, Deacon Harris's dead body was surrounded by a pool of blood. He died the same way the Simmses had died—by a hail of bullets. The Bible verses that Sister Mathis had quoted to him had come back to haunt him.

"An evil man seeks only rebellion: therefore a cruel messenger will be sent against him." The messengers came. And now Deacon Harris's dead body lay slumped on the floor with both of his eyes wide open.

Wynnefield, Philadelphia

Craig's gray Mercedes pulled up in front of Frank's parents' house in Wynnefield. The street was quiet and filled with tall trees.

"You want me to come with you?" Craig asked.

"No, I'll be fine," Frank replied as he opened the door and got out of the car.

Graveyard pulled up and parked his car right behind Craig. They had just gotten back to the city an hour earlier from their trip out to LA. Both men sat inside their cars watching as Frank opened the front door and walked inside.

Frank closed the door and just stood there looking around. This was the first time since his parents' deaths that he'd been back to the house. A strange chill entered his body. Then past memories filled his mind. This was the house that Frank grew up in, the house where his parents gave him all the love they could. After a long sigh, Frank walked up the stairs. He walked down the narrow hallway and entered his parents' bedroom. The bed was made and everything inside was organized neatly. Frank walked over to his father's dresser and opened the bottom drawer. He reached past a few white T-shirts and quickly found what he was looking for.

Inside his hand was his father's personal journal. As long as Frank could remember, his father had kept one. It was a habit for his father to always write down things that were on his mind. As his father got older, he started forgetting more and more things, so the journal came in handy.

Frank walked over and sat down on the edge of the bed. He opened the large black book and started flipping through the pages. The journal was filled with years of personal thoughts. Frank turned the page to the last Sunday his father was alive. The page was empty. Frank then turned to the Thursday before his parents' deaths. The page had just a few lines of writing on it. Frank began to read.

I don't know what's going on with Deacon Harris, but lately he's been acting mighty strange. He don't know, but I saw the two pretty girls pass him a bag a few days ago. One was tall and white, and the other looked as if she could be Asian. I hope everything is all right. I know something is wrong, 'cause he don't hardly look at me in the eyes no more. But like I do every day, I'll pray for him.

Frank quickly flipped the page to Saturday.

The Deacon finally came around to acting like his old self again. He told me he had a few family issues to fix. I don't think it was the whole truth, but at least we are speaking again. He suggested that me and

Clara stand out in front of the church tomorrow and take some pictures with some of the new church members. Strange, but I told him we would. Even though we're speaking again, I can still tell that something ain't right with the deacon. But like I do every day, I'll pray for him.

At that moment Frank knew that Deacon Harris had something to do with his parents being murdered. Through his father's writing, he had discovered the real truth. Deacon Harris had set up his parents to be killed. And Frank was sure that somehow Vega, his number one enemy, was behind it all.

Frank stood from the bed and rushed out of the bedroom. The large black journal was clutched inside his hand. When he got back into Craig's car, he said, "I need you to get to my father's church fast!"

"Why, what's up?" Craig asked while starting up the car and pulling off down the street.

Frank looked at Craig and saw the concerned look on his face. "Deacon Harris had my father set up! It's all in my father's journal."

"What!" Craig asked in total disbelief.

"Somehow Vega got to him and he paid the deacon to set up my parents to be killed!"

Craig couldn't believe his ears. As he maneuvered the car through traffic, he looked over at Frank and said, "That's why the deacon's been acting so strange lately."

"Exactly! He knows what he did, and his conscience has been eating him alive."

Craig drove down Fifty-fourth Street, still in total shock. "But why would the deacon set up your parents?" he asked.

"That's what we are about to find out."

While Craig continued to drive toward the church, Frank sat there with his head down. Craig looked through the rearview mirror and saw that Graveyard's tinted black Dodge Magnum was following closely behind them, right where he was supposed to be.

Southwest Philly

When Junie walked into the house, he found Vega sitting on the sofa between his two gorgeous sex slaves. Junie walked over and whispered something into his ear. Whatever the news was, it brought a big smile to Vega's face.

"Where are they now?" Vega asked.

"I don't know. They asked me to drop them off at the train. You know them two. They probably walking around the park picking flowers by now," Junie said and laughed.

Vega stood from the sofa with both women wrapped around his arms. "Good work, unc. I'll be upstairs if you need me," Vega said as he and his two sex kittens walked over to the stairs and started to climb the steps.

When Craig pulled his Mercedes onto the block where the church was located, shocked looks covered both of their faces. Three police cars and an ambulance were all parked outside the church along with a large crowd of nosey spectators. A line of yellow tape was tied across the front of the church doors. People stood around crying and shaking their heads in total disbelief. In less than one week another member of their church was dead.

Frank got out of the car and ran into the crowd. Graveyard was right behind him with his loaded .40 caliber tucked inside his pants.

"What happened?" Frank asked the first face he recognized. It was his mother's good friend, Sister Mathis.

"Frank, somebody killed him!" she said as tears rolled down her face.

"Killed who?"

"Deacon Harris! Somebody shot him this morning, right outside your father's office!"

"Damn!" Frank said as he slowly turned around and walked away.

Philadelphia Federal Detention Center, Unit 5-South

The two federal informants were housed on the fifth floor. None of the other FDC inmates knew about their secret meetings and phone conversations with the two FBI agents. The informants had also met with a representative from the federal prosecutor's office, and they were now waiting to give their sworn statements. Although what they would say was all lies, it would be enough to start a full-fledged investigation on Frank's Underworld drug empire. And the lies would take eighteen years off both of their sentences.

Anthony and Kevin both stood on the top tier, watching as the other inmates sat around playing cards or basketball, and crowded around the phones. Anthony pulled Kevin to a secluded corner on the tier. "Look, homie, once we tell these people what they wanna hear, we'll be out of prison in a heartbeat," he said.

"What if they find out that most of the stuff we said are lies?" Kevin asked.

"They won't! The feds want Underworld bad. That's all their investigation is really about—taking him down. So why not make up lies about the man? Who knows if Underworld had anything to do with Vega's parents dying in that car crash a few years ago.

Who cares? All I'm saying, homie, is let's keep feeding them bullshit as long as they keep eating it."

"What if Underworld finds out about us? I heard that the man got people everywhere! Maybe he even got people on his payroll inside here," Kevin said, looking around the tier.

"Don't believe that shit, Kev! Underworld is a whole lot of hype. Why do you think nobody knows about us and what we've been doing for the feds? Anyway, fuck 'im. It's either him or us. And once we give the grand jury our statements next week, it will be over for both Vega and Underworld," Anthony said confidently.

Kevin looked at Anthony's serious expression and started grinning. "You're right, homie. It's either them or us," he said as they both started walking down the tier.

As the two men walked along the top tier, they never noticed the set of brown eyes that had been closely watching their every move. For the last few days, the two men were being monitored closely by a few anonymous watchers who were waiting for the perfect opportunity to strike.

Chapter 19

Underworld Entertainment

Cassie, Riley, and Valerie all got off the elevator and headed toward the main conference room. When they entered the empty room, they each found a seat. Valerie quickly pulled out a pencil and pad and Riley already had his laptop up and running.

"All of our artists will do two songs each for the Underworld compilation album. The project should be completed by mid November," Cassie said.

"How many videos do you plan on doing for the project?" Riley asked.

"At least two, but we'll just play it by ear."

"How soon do you want us to start promoting the new album?" Valerie asked.

"As soon as possible. Val, you make sure we get full-page advertisements for the next three months in *Ozone*, *Source*, *XXL*, *King*, *Vibe*, and *Smooth* magazines. Also make sure you get with our West Coast, Midwest, down South, and East Coast publicists and street teams. I want this new project to be just as big as Diddy did with his Bad Boy compilation album. So make sure you do a major press release and get in contact with our friends in radio. Make sure they all get an advance copy of the new album. Oh, and don't forget the people over at Satellite radio."

"I won't," Val said, writing down everything.

"Anything else?" Riley asked as he typed into his computer.

"Yeah. I would like a few features on the album."

"Like who?" Riley asked as he looked up.

"The best of the best!"

"I'm on it," Riley said.

"I'll make a few calls and see if I can get Janell Jones to sing on one of our artist's tracks," Cassie said.

Riley and Valerie both stopped what they were doing and looked up.

"Janell Jones!" they both said in unison.

"She's like the biggest star in the world right now," Valerie said enthusiastically. "I bought all of her albums."

"Do you really think Underworld Entertainment can get Janell Jones on one of the artist's tracks?" Riley asked.

"I think I can make that happen," Cassie said confidently as she looked at both of their excited faces.

"Do you know what kind of numbers the album will do if you get Janell Jones on a track? She's one of the biggest artists in the world. I'm talking major! Mary, Mariah, Janet, Beyoncé major!" Riley said excitedly.

"Well we talked already, and I suggested that she do a song with J-Dawg," Cassie said.

"That would be fantastic!" Valerie said. "I'm talking platinum single with the right radio push behind it."

"When did you see her, Cassie?" Riley asked.

"Last night in LA."

"Oh, at one of those private industry parties that we never get to go to," Valerie said with a grin.

Cassie stood and said, "Something like that."

Then she winked and walked out of the room smiling from ear to ear.

Later that evening

The long green snake slithered around Spade's naked body. She loved the way it felt. Lying on the floor of her bedroom, surrounded by candles, her man, and her snake was the ultimate pleasure for Spade, especially after committing another murder and getting away with it. As soon as they entered their house, they added Deacon Harris's name to their long list of murder victims. He was victim number fourteen.

Spade rolled over on her back and spread open her legs. A devilish grin was plastered on her beautiful face. Canon sat up and stared at her flawless, petite body, admiring everything about her. Spade had rings inside her tongue, nose, ears, navel, and vagina lips. Black nail polish covered her fingernails and toenails, and religious tattoos covered her arms and breasts.

"Come to paradise," she said seductively.

Canon crawled on top of her body and started nibbling around her neck. He then placed both of her legs onto his broad shoulders and slid his manhood deep into the wetness of her inviting paradise.

Frank was disgusted. Someone had killed the deacon before he could get any answers about his parents' deaths. Craig sat on the sofa inside his condominium, watching Frank pace across the floor.

"That no good sonofabitch had my parents set up to be killed!" Frank snapped. "I was in Miami when my father wanted to tell me what was going on. He called when I was out taking care of business with Mr. Sanchez. Cassie talked to him."

"What did he say?" Craig asked.

"He told Cassie that there was something important he needed to talk to me face to face about. I'm almost positive that it was about Deacon Harris's strange behavior."

"Why would the deacon do something like this?" Craig asked as he sat back shaking his head.

"Money! Power! Respect! Everything my father had that he didn't. Vega will pay for this! He and everything he loves will pay for all the hurt and pain he has caused me! Where's Graveyard?" Frank asked.

"He's out checking on all the addresses on the list," Craig said.

"Good. I'm tired of playing this game with Vega. By next week I want Vega and everything associated with him dead and destroyed."

"Don't worry. Graveyard is on it. And I made sure he'll have a few of our top men with him to help things go smoothly," Craig said as he stood.

After a long sigh Frank stepped out onto the balcony and Craig joined him. The scene from high above gave them a perfect view of the city. Both men stood there lost in their own thoughts.

"When this all over, Frank, we can move on and continue with our blueprint for success and wealth."

Frank looked deep into his best friend's eyes and said, "Craig, success and wealth are not my main objectives in life. Power is. Once a person has enough power, he can control the wealthiest people in the world."

The Four Seasons Hotel, Beverly Hills

Janell lay across the bed inside her elegant private suite. Her manager and one of her publicists had lost the battle and left the room. They were both trying to convince her to go to another private industry party. But Janell was tired. Her non-stop sexual workout with Craig had her body feeling fatigued and drained. Plus she was fed up with being around all the superficial industry people. Hearing the same stories and seeing all the same phony smiles was nerve-racking.

There were just a few people in the entertainment industry that Janell considered real, down-to-earth friends. And Cassie was one of them. She had enjoyed their conversation the night before. It wasn't the same old celebrity gossip that she was used to hearing, like who was sleeping with who, and who was about to become the next big thing. Her conversation with Cassie was real.

Janell loved her fans more than anything, but so many times she wished she could be a regular person again. Being with Craig made her feel regular and appreciated, and not the big superstar that everyone else saw.

Janell reached for the remote control to the flat screen TV. She turned to BET, and to her surprise, her new video for the song "Love Can't Wait" was playing. She laid back on one of the thick quilted pillows and smiled. She had written the song just for Craig. And every time she heard the poignant lyrics, a swarm of unknown chills entered her body, causing her to shiver.

Center City, Philadelphia

Artie Fletcher was a cop on a serious mission. And he was determined to let nothing nor no one stand in his way. After finding an empty place to park the stolen car that he was driving, Artie took out his cell phone and dialed a number.

"Underworld Entertainment. How can I help you?" a female's voice asked.

"My name is Douglas Price. I'm the new assistant program director at Power 99 FM. Is Ms. Cassie Lopez available by any chance?"

"Hold one minute," the lady said as she put him on hold.

A few moments later, Cassie picked up the phone and said, "Hello. This is Cassie Lopez. How can I help you?"

Then the line went dead. After Artie hung up the cell phone he reclined in his seat and started smiling. His 9 mm pistol was underneath his shirt, fully loaded. Artie looked at his gold watch and saw that the time was eight forty-eight PM. He knew that the sky would soon be turning black. For him, nighttime was the perfect time to kill. And Cassie Lopez, Frank Simms's beautiful fiancée was the next person to die.

Chapter 20

Thirty-fifth Street, West Philadelphia

BUTCHER PULLED UP IN FRONT of a small row house and beeped the horn. A brown-skinned man walked out the front door and got inside Butcher's red Lexus. Butcher quickly pulled off.

"Yo, what's up, Pervis?" Butcher asked.

"Butcher, shit is getting real fucked up, homie," Pervis said, taking out a rolled up blunt of purple haze.

After Pervis lit up the blunt, he rolled down the window and started smoking.

"Don't worry, Pervis. Me and Vega is handling something real important right now. As soon as shit gets right, you'll be taken care of," Butcher said as he drove his car past the Philadelphia Zoo.

"Man, I hope y'all hurry up, 'cause shit is looking real bad for us now that we ain't been selling no drugs the last few days. Man, what the hell is going on?" Pervis asked as he passed Butcher the blunt.

"Somebody knocked off our drug connect a few days ago."

"What! So that's what it is?" Pervis asked, clearly shocked.

"Don't worry, Pervis. As soon as me and Vega take care of some other major issues, we're gonna get us a new drug connect and start hitting you back off again. Just keep laying low for a while," Butcher said as he blew out a thick cloud of gray smoke.

"Do this major business got anything to do with Underworld?" Pervis asked.

Butcher looked over at his young friend and smiled. Then he passed Pervis the blunt. "Everything has to do with Underworld," Butcher said. "The nigga is in our way. He has to go!"

Pervis inhaled the blunt and blew out a cloud of smoke through his nose. "Underworld ain't no average Joe," Pervis said. "He and his street crew is major!"

"What did you hear?" Butcher asked as he stopped his car at a red light on Girard Avenue.

"I heard that the dude Underworld got lawyers, judges, cops, and all kinds of people on his payroll. I still can't believe that Frank Simms, the owner of Underworld Entertainment is the same person who's the boss of the Philly Underworld drug movement," Pervis said as he took another hit on the blunt.

"Yeah, that's him all right. Suge Knight, Russell Simmons and John Gotti all rolled up in one," Butcher said as the light turned green and he pulled off.

"Well fuck 'im! I'm with you 100 percent, Butcher! I hope you and Vega take his fucking head off." Pervis laughed. He was now feeling the effects of the marijuana.

"Don't you worry, Pervis. By next week Underworld will be a distant memory, and the city will be ours."

Pervis reclined back into the comfortable leather seats and smiled. Butcher was still talking, but Pervis wasn't hearing one word. The purple haze had him lost in another place and time.

The Marriott, Downtown Philadelphia

Graveyard had just returned to his room at the Marriott. After driving around the city all day long, he was finally ready to enjoy himself. He'd driven by every piece of property that was on the list. Now not only did he know about every spot that Vega owned, but he also knew about the house where Vega laid his head at night. Graveyard knew that Vega wasn't the sharp street guy that he thought he was. By putting all of his properties in his own name, Vega had put his family and friends in great danger. This was a war. And now everyone that Vega loved was standing out on the front line without any shield to protect them.

After Graveyard called Frank and told him everything he'd found out, Frank was very pleased. Now it was only a matter of time before the mighty Vega and everything around him would crumble.

After a long, refreshing, hot shower, Graveyard dried himself off and slid on his silk boxers. He lay across the bed, satisfied with how his long day had turned out. As soon as he got comfortable in bed, the knock on the door made him jump up. Graveyard got out of bed and walked over to the door. He didn't bother to look out the peephole because he already knew who it was.

When he opened the door three beautiful black women stood there smiling at him. After they walked inside the room and closed the door, they all started getting undressed. Graveyard stood back with his arms crossed and an excited look on his face.

"Underworld told us to take real, real good care of you," one of the women said.

Graveyard walked over and laid on the bed. Moments later the three naked women joined him. Tonight he had his hands full. And DNA was gonna make sure it would be a night to remember.

Frank was driving his BMW home. The news that Graveyard had told him had been the highlight of his stressful day. Everything was now in motion. Frank knew that Vega was the person behind Deacon Harris's murder. He knew that Vega had him killed so Frank wouldn't get any answers out of him. But now Frank wouldn't need the deacon for any answers. Because of Graveyard, Frank had all the answers he needed.

After leaving Craig, Frank called Cassie and told her that he would meet her back at home. As he drove his car on the I-76, Frank couldn't help but think about the deacon being murdered. Frank felt no sadness in his heart. Something had been telling him all along that the deacon had played a major part in his parents' brutal slayings. Frank was a true believer in karma. What comes around, goes around, and it all came back to Deacon Harris.

Delaware Avenue

Craig sat on the sofa enjoying the smooth, soulful voice of Jaheem. Scented candles filled the air in his living room. After eating and taking a long, hot shower, it was now time for him to kick back and relax. Good music was his escape from it all.

The sound of his ringing cell phone interrupted his peaceful mood. Craig grabbed his phone from the coffee table. When he saw the name and number on the ID screen, he quickly answered.

"So your love really can't wait," he said.

"Nope, and after my tour is over, you're gonna find out just how much it can't," Janell said into the phone.

"No Hollywood parties tonight?"

"Nope. Just me, my vibrating toy, and you," Janell said as they both started laughing.

Underworld Entertainment

"Cassie, can you give me a ride home?" Valerie asked as she ran behind her on the elevators.

"Where's Riley?"

"He already left," Valerie said.

"Sure, but you're driving," Cassie said as she pressed the button for the ground floor garage. "I'm beat."

After they stepped off the elevator, Cassie and Valerie got into Cassie's brand new Jaguar. The car was a present from Frank. Cassie sat in the passenger seat and Valerie got behind the wheel. Valerie had driven the car many times before, usually when Cassie didn't feel like driving.

Valerie started up the car, turned on the radio, and pulled out of the garage parking lot. Then she eased out into the downtown traffic. The sky was pitch black with a half moon and just a few stars. Cassie reclined way back in her seat and got herself more relaxed. Valerie kept her eyes on the road straight ahead, enjoying the sounds from the radio. She couldn't wait to get home to her boyfriend Leon and their cat Tickles.

On the corner of Broad and Spring Garden streets Valerie stopped at a red light. She never paid attention to the black Chrysler that slowly pulled up beside her. When Valerie finally looked over at the car, she saw the black man inside pointing a gun right at her head. Before she realized what was going on, the bullets from the man's 9 mm pistol were already exploding from the gun.

Boom! Boom! Boom! Boom! Boom! Boom! Boom! Boom!

Eight bullets shattered through the window and door of the car. Then the black Chrysler quickly sped off and disappeared into the darkness of the August night. People inside their cars quickly jumped out to check on the two passengers inside the bullet riddled Jaguar. A small crowd stood around the car, looking at the two females lying inside. Glass was shattered and one woman was screaming hysterically while the other lay still.

Moments later two police cars pulled up at the scene and the officers got out and rushed over to the two female victims. When officer Roy Cooper saw that one of the women inside the car was Frank "Underworld" Simms's fiancée, he couldn't believe his eyes.

"Oh, shit!" he mumbled.

CHAPTER 21

AFTER DRIVING A FEW BLOCKS away from the scene, Detective Artie Fletcher parked the stolen car across the street from an Amoco gas station. Then he calmly got out of the car, shut the door, and walked away. About two blocks from the gas station, not too far from the Philadelphia Community College campus, Artie walked down a small, quiet street and got into his car. Moments later he drove off with a huge smile plastered across his face. Artie quickly pulled out his cell phone and started dialing numbers. He couldn't wait to tell Vega the good news.

Officer Cooper watched as the two women were laid on stretchers and placed inside waiting ambulances. A police tow truck waited to move the bullet-riddled car while a few witnesses stood around being questioned by police officers. After the two ambulances drove off, Officer Cooper took out his cell phone and quickly called Frank. When the voice mail came on, he left an urgent message.

Vega, Homicide, Junie, and Butcher were all waiting inside the house when Artie arrived. Vega had called Spade and Canon, but neither of them answered the phone. Artie sat down on the sofa and looked around at all the excited faces.

"I got that bitch good!" he said.

"Who?" Butcher asked.

"Cassie! I drove up on her at a red light and almost emptied my whole clip on her ass! Somebody else was lying back on the passenger seat, and I'm sure I hit her a few times too! But one thing for sure is that Cassie Lopez is one dead bitch!"

"When did you set this up?" Vega asked.

"I've been posted outside Underworld Entertainment all day long. I used a stolen car to do the hit. My car was parked a few blocks away."

"Are you sure she's dead?" Vega asked, his eyes wide with excitement.

"I'm not 100 percent, but I'll tell you this much, if she ain't dead, she will be soon." Artie laughed.

"This is good! This is real good!" Vega stood from the sofa. "I hope you're right, Artie. If so you'll get your one-hundred-thousand-dollar reward as soon as possible. Tonight we'll just all sit around and wait for the late night news to come on. I'm sure this will be the major story of the day. Ms. Cassie Lopez, President of Underworld Entertainment, shot dead inside her car," Vega said as everyone stood and started laughing.

"And Underworld and Craig are next," Homicide added.

Vega walked over to the wall and turned on the large plasma TV.

"We got a little while till news time," he said as he sat back down on the sofa.

West Philly

"One must die for another one to live," Spade said as she stood there feeding her snake, Hulk, small white mice. Canon watched in excitement. For them, seeing the snake kill its prey was a wonderful thrill.

Spade turned to Canon and said, "I believe that when a life is taken away, it's replaced instantly by another life. The fourteen people that we have killed have all been replaced by newborns. Death is life," she said as she reached out and grabbed Canon's hands.

"Death is life," Canon repeated, then leaned forward and gave Spade a long passionate kiss.

They walked over to the bed and sat down. The cell phone on top of the nightstand was ringing, but neither one paid it any mind. Spade looked deeply into Canon's eyes and said, "I feel that soon our time in this world will be coming to an end, just like all the people that we killed. But remember, my love, we will accept death whenever it comes, because death is life."

"Death is life," Canon said as they began kissing once again.

Hahnemann University Hospital

Frank, Craig, and Graveyard rushed through the emergency room glass doors. After Frank listened to Cooper's urgent message on his voice mail, he rushed to the hospital. On his way there he called Craig and Graveyard to meet him. When Frank saw one of the doctors, he ran up to him and said, "Doc! Doc, is Cassie Lopez all right?"

Before the doctor could respond, Cassie, Riley, and J-Dawg all walked into the crowded room. Cassie had her left arm bandaged. Frank quickly rushed over to her and they embraced in a long hug. Tears fell from both of their eyes.

"I love you so much, Frank," Cassie said as she remained wrapped inside his arms. Everyone stood back watching the emotional scene.

"What happened?" Frank asked, looking into her watery eyes.

"It happened so fast, Frank! I was lying back in the passenger seat resting when I heard the gunshots go off.

All I remember is feeling a sting in my arm and protecting myself from all the shattered glass. I'm fine. I was only grazed by a bullet and have some minor cuts from the glass, but . . . but . . . but . . ."
"But what! What happened to Valerie?"
"Frank, Val was shot six times, once in the face. She's still in surgery. Her blood was all over my clothes, Frank. It was terrible!"
"Are you OK?"
"I'm fine, Frank, but I'm worried about Valerie. She's in that operating room because of me. Whoever tried to kill her was after me! And the only reason I'm not the one being operated on is because I let her drive my car," Cassie said as the flow of tears escaped the confines of her eyes. "If she dies, Frank, her death was meant for me!" Cassie said, laying her head on his chest.

Everyone stood around speechless amidst the chaos of the emergency room. Frank pulled Cassie to the side.

"Baby, I'm truly sorry. Don't worry. I'm gonna get the person who did this to y'all. I promise," Frank said. "Until I get this problem fixed, I'll have you under twenty-four-hour protection. And it will all be fixed very soon."

"Frank, baby, I'm fine. It's Valerie I'm worried about. She's my good friend and now she's laying up in surgery because of me," Cassie said as tears again started falling from her eyes.

Frank reached out and wiped away her tears with his hand. "It's not because of you," he said. "It's my fault! And I'm gonna fix it. I swear!"

After Frank and Cassie embraced in another long hug, they walked over and sat down inside the emergency room waiting area. Graveyard and four of Frank's top men were standing around talking outside the emergency room entrance. Craig, Riley, and J-

Dawg were all seated together talking amongst themselves.

Suddenly a swarm of news reporters and photographers all rushed through the large glass doors. Before Cassie and Frank could do anything, the cameras and microphones were all up in their faces.

"Is it true, Ms. Lopez, that someone tried to take your life tonight?" a reporter yelled.

"How many times were you shot?" a female reporter asked.

"Mr. Simms, does this have anything to do with the recent murders of your parents, and the murder of Deacon Harris earlier today?" another reporter asked.

The scene inside the hospital was chaotic as Frank and Cassie tried to shield themselves from the boisterous crowd. The hospital security team quickly showed up and began pushing the crowd of news reporters and photographers out the door. Frank and Cassie were quickly escorted into another section of the hospital. Everyone inside the hospital was staring at them. Because of their successful entertainment company, almost everyone in Philadelphia knew who they were.

Frank had his arm wrapped around Cassie's shoulders. A rage was boiling deep inside his soul. He knew that Vega was the man behind the assassination attempt on his fiancée, and the reason why his parents were now dead and buried. After Frank and Cassie sat down on an empty bench, Cassie laid her head across his lap. Frank started running his hand through her long hair. At that moment Cassie felt more safe than she ever had before. She knew that Frank wouldn't hesitate to give up his life for her, and Cassie felt the same way.

As thoughts began clouding Frank's head, all he could think about was Vega. And executing the ultimate revenge.

***

Agents Mitchell and Stokes sat inside their car, right across the street from the hospital.

"What the hell is going on, Stokes?" Mitchell asked, slamming down his fist on the dashboard. "In less than one week, Frank's parents are murdered right outside their church. The Deacon was murdered earlier today inside the church. And now someone does a drive-by shooting on Frank's fiancée!"

"Whatever it is, he must've really pissed off somebody! I wouldn't be surprised if Vega's behind it all. Everyone who knows the two men also knows how much they can't stand each other. Ever since Vega's younger brother Tony was found with his head cut off, it's been an all out war between them. At least that's what our jailhouse informants keep telling us."

"But Vega knows he can't win a drug war against Frank. That's like committing suicide."

"Maybe Vega knows something that we don't know," Stokes said. "One thing for sure, when we send our informants in next week, we're gonna start finding out a whole lot more about these two ruthless men."

"Well as soon as we find what we need to get an indictment on these two, it's off to life in federal prison for both of them." Mitchell laughed.

While the two agents sat inside their car talking, Graveyard stood on the side of the newspaper stand watching them very closely. After the two agents pulled off down the street, he calmly walked back inside the hospital.

Southwest Philly

Everyone inside Vega's house was waiting for the Fox late night news to come on. Finally the news reporter looked into the camera and said, "Today's top story is the assassination attempt on Cassie Lopez. Details are still sketchy, but witnesses on the scene told us that an African-American male pulled up beside her late model Jaguar and started shooting. It all took place on the corner of Broad and Spring Garden streets. The gunman shot up the vehicle and quickly sped off in an unidentified black car. Ironically, Ms. Lopez was only grazed by one of the eight bullets that entered her vehicle. At the time of the shooting Ms. Lopez was lying back in the passenger seat while her secretary, Ms. Valerie Jackson, was driving. Our Fox news reporters at the hospital have told us that Ms. Jackson is still in surgery. As you all may know, Ms. Cassie Lopez is the president of Underworld Entertainment, and the fiancée of Frank „Underworld' Simms, the owner of—"

Vega cut off the TV and slammed the remote control on the floor. "Goddamit! The bitch is still alive!" he shouted.

Artie just sat there shaking his head in total disbelief. He still couldn't believe what he had just heard. "I can't believe this shit!" he said as he stood. "I thought the bitch was Cassie!"

Vega stood and walked over to him. "Don't worry, Artie. You tried. We'll get 'em sooner or later," he said, patting Artie on his shoulder. Vega then walked over to a closet and went inside. When he walked back out he had a large stack of money in his hand. "Here," he said, tossing the money to Artie. Artie caught the stack of bills in mid air. "That's ten grand. At least somebody got shot tonight," he said as a smile spread across his face.

Baltimore, Maryland

Outside one of West Baltimore's hottest nightclubs, Tadpole and two of his closet friends stood around talking to a group of beautiful, young females. Parked just a few feet away was his brand new set of wheels—a dark blue Bentley Continental GTC worth one hundred ninety thousand dollars. Tadpole and his crew were all well respected hustlers throughout the city of Baltimore. At just twenty-six-years-old, Tadpole was already one of the most successful young hustlers in the city, all because of his favorite older cousin Frank "Underworld" Simms.

Parked on the opposite side of the street, two men sat inside a gold Lexus coupe, closely watching Tadpole. Muscle and Terry were two well known stickup boys and kidnappers. For six months the two men had been plotting on kidnapping Tadpole, knowing that they could earn a large ransom for his safe return.

"Yo, we gotta get that pretty boy ass nigga soon!" Muscle said. Muscle was a large, muscular man with a dark chocolate complexion and an ugly face.

"Yo, don't worry, yo, we will, and when we do, we taking nothing less than a million dollars to give back his punk ass," Terry said with a evil grin.

Terry was another dark complexioned man, but a lot shorter than Muscle. Out of the two of them, Terry was considered the brains. Muscle was just what his name implied—the muscle.

"I heard that Tadpole is somehow related to the guy Underworld," Muscle said.

"Fuck Underworld, yo. Who da fuck is this Underworld dude that everybody be talking about? His name has been floating around for years, but why don't nobody know who fuck he is?" Terry asked.

"I heard that he's some Jamaican guy from D.C. And I also heard that he's the black guy who owns that record company in Philly. You know, yo, the rap label," Muscle said.

"Yo, don't believe everything you hear out on these streets. Whoever this guy Underworld is, believe me he ain't no Jamaican or no wannabe Suge Knight. And to be totally honest, yo, he might not be real. If the nigga was all who the streets say he is, the feds woulda been grabbed his ass," Terry said confidently.

"Yo, I'm just telling you about the rumors I heard," Muscle said.

"Yo, fuck that fantasy shit about some mysterious unknown Underworld nigga! That nigga over there is reality," Terry said, pointing his finger out the window toward Tadpole. "Once we catch his ass slipping, yo, he's ours. And if the rumors are true and he's this Underworld dude's real family, we gonna charge two million to give him back." Terry laughed. "Underworld, ha . . . ha . . . ha . . . What is this world coming to?" Terry asked as he started up the car and slowly drove down the street.

Chapter 22

AFTER ARTIE LEFT THE HOUSE and went home, Butcher, Junie, Homicide, and Vega all gathered around and started talking.

"I wanted to tell everybody here that I'm meeting with a new drug connect tomorrow afternoon," Vega said.

"You found somebody who can meet our demands?" Butcher asked.

"Yeah, I've been putting things together for the last few days."

"Who is it?" Butcher asked.

"It's Cindy's older brother," Vega said.

"I didn't know that Cindy had a brother," Butcher said.

"Me either until a few days ago. She told me after one of our wild sexcapades. But there's more to it."

"What's that?" Homicide asked.

"Her brother has a problem with Frank also." Vega grinned as he looked around at everyone's faces.

"Who is he?" Butcher asked.

After a long sigh Vega said, "Cindy's brother is Bobby Chang!"

"Bobby Chang!" Butcher yelled. "Cindy is Bobby Chang's lil sister?"

"Yup," Vega answered. "And his only sister," he added.

Homicide and Junie both stood there with dumbfounded looks. Neither of them had ever heard of Bobby Chang.

"Well tell us who this Bobby Chang is," Junie said.

Vega stood from the sofa and yelled upstairs for Cindy to come down. Moments later the short, Asian beauty walked downstairs. Cindy was dressed in a matching all black Victoria's Secret bra and panty set with a pair of black three-inch Gucci wrap-around heels. She walked over to Vega and stood by his side.

"Yes, daddy what is it?" she asked.

"Turn around for me."

After Cindy turned around, Vega lifted up her long hair to display the small tattoo on the back of her neck. The tattoo was a picture of a red dragon with the initials A.M.F. written underneath.

"Go back upstairs with Jewell," Vega said after releasing her hair.

Even after viewing the tattoo, Homicide and Junie still had no clue who Cindy really was. All they knew about her was that she was an attractive Asian woman who enjoyed black dick and white pussy.

But her tattoo told Butcher all he needed to know. He stood back smiling from ear to ear.

Vega stared into Homicide's and Junie's curious eyes and said, "Gentlemen, Cindy's older brother is Bobby Chang, and Bobby Chang is the boss of A.M.F.—The Asian Mafia Family!"

Big smiles appeared on Homicide's and Junie's stunned faces. They now knew that if all went well, Vega had struck a gold mine.

Hahnemann University Hospital
Early Sunday morning

After the doctors performed a successful surgery on Valerie, she was taken to the ICU where she was listed in critical condition. Valerie had been shot six times—once in the mouth, once in the stomach, twice in the left shoulder, and twice in the left hip. Luckily none of the bullets hit any vital organs. By the grace of God she had survived the assassination attempt that was originally planned for Cassie.

Before everyone left to go home, Graveyard told Frank about the two agents he had seen snooping around. After Frank whispered something to him and Craig, they all walked out the hospital. Four of Franks top men stood around like a trained military combat unit. They watched as a tinted black limousine pulled up and parked. The news reporters and photographers had all left, so now the coast was clear. Everyone watched as Frank and Cassie climbed into the back of the limo and closed the door. When the limo drove off, they all got into their cars and went their separate ways.

"I love you," Cassie said as she lay wrapped in Frank's arms.

Frank smiled and kissed her softly on the lips. "I love you too, but that was a close call. I could've lost you."

"God got much bigger plans for us. That's why he saved us," Cassie said softly.

"I'm just happy that you and Val both came out of this mess alive. I don't know what I would do if I ever lost you."

"Us!" Cassie yelled.

"Yeah, Val too," Frank said.

"I'm not talking about Val," Cassie said as she looked directly into Frank's eyes.

"Then who is us?" Frank asked.

"Me and our unborn baby."

Shock instantly appeared on Frank's face. "What baby?" he asked.

"Our baby, silly. The one I've been carrying for four weeks."

"You're pregnant!" Frank said and sat up, his eyes wide with excitement. "When . . . how . . ."

"The doctor told me back at the hospital. I found out right before you got there. I wanted to wait till we were all alone to tell you the good news," Cassie said.

"Are you sure?" Frank asked.

"I'm positive, baby. The doctor checked me while I was getting my arm looked over. He said that I was around four weeks pregnant and that our baby was not harmed at all."

Frank couldn't believe his own ears. He and Cassie had been trying to have a baby for over a year. Although excitement showed on his face, deep inside Frank was very upset that someone had tried to take her life and the life of his unborn child.

"I don't want you to go back to work until I get this situation fixed," he told Cassie.

"No, Frank! I'm not gonna stop doing what I do!"

"But—"

Cassie put her fingers to his lips and said, "You just provide me with some tight security. I'll be fine. I have a job to do and I'm gonna do it. Just promise me one thing."

"What's that?" Frank asked.

"That you're gonna end all this madness soon."

"I promise," Frank said as Cassie relaxed across his lap with a big smile on her face. "I promise," he said softly.

Sunday Afternoon

"Honey, are you OK?" Artie's wife, Pat, asked.

"Yeah, yeah, I'm fine. I'll see you and the kids later. Now go and enjoy church," he said as he sat up on the edge of the bed.

Pat walked over to her husband and softly kissed him on the lips.

"I'll see you later. I love you," she said.

"I love you too," Artie said as he watched her walk out of the bedroom and close the door.

Artie was disappointed. After learning that both women had survived his assassination attempt, it made him even more upset with himself. He was almost positive that the woman he did shoot hadn't survived his close range 9 mm attack. Artie reached under the bed and pulled out his loaded .44 Magnum.

"The next time I get a crack at one of those motherfuckers, there won't be no mistakes. Or survivors," Artie said.

Chestnut Hill

Frank and Cassie were sitting at the kitchen table talking when Frank's cell phone started vibrating on his hip. He pulled out the phone and answered after checking the caller ID.

"I planned on calling you soon," Frank said.

"I need to see you as soon as possible," the caller said. "How fast can you get here?"

"I'm on my way now," Frank replied when he noticed the urgency in the man's voice. "Is everything OK?"

"I hope so. I'll see you when you get down here. Bye."

Cassie looked at Frank and noticed the worried look on his face. "Baby, you OK?" she asked.

"I'm fine," Frank said as he stood and walked around the table.

"Who was that?" Cassie asked.

After a long sigh, Frank said, "That was Mr. Sanchez. He wants to see me."

"Is everything OK?"

"I'm not sure, but whatever it is, he wants to talk about it now!" Frank looked Cassie in the eyes and said, "I'll be back soon."

After rubbing her stomach, they kissed each other long and passionately. He then dialed Craig's phone number and waited.

"What's up?" Craig asked when he answered.

"Meet me at the airport in a half hour. I'll explain everything on the jet."

After Frank closed his cell phone, he kissed Cassie one more time and rushed out of the kitchen. When Cassie heard the front door shut, a flow of tears started falling from her eyes. This was the part of the ruthless drug game that she hated most. Every time Frank rushed out to another emergency call, it scared her. She knew that the streets had love for no one. And even though Frank was the man that he was, there were no guarantees that he would ever walk back through the door.

CHAPTER 23

Chinatown

Even for a Sunday afternoon it wasn't unusual for Asian venders to be lined up and down the sidewalks. People walked around shopping and talking while small Asian children ran up and down the streets like there wasn't a care in the world. And for most of them, there wasn't. Asians always took good care of their own, helping out a poor, struggling family until the family was on its feet again and able to pay back its debt. Another thing that the Asian community didn't do was call on outside authorities to come in and fix its internal problems. When there was a problem, they had lots of ways to fix it themselves.

The white Cadillac truck pulled up in front of the large Chinese restaurant on Eighth Street. Junie sat behind the wheel watching as Vega, Butcher, and Cindy all exited the vehicle and walked inside the restaurant. Once they disappeared from his view, he slowly pulled off.

When the group walked into the restaurant, it was crowded with customers. Asians, blacks, and whites all sat around at their tables, enjoying their meals. A short, attractive Asian woman walked up to Cindy and kissed her on both cheeks. After saying a few words in their native Chinese language, Cindy, Vega, and Butcher followed the women straight to the back of the restaurant. Once they reached the back of the restaurant, the woman approached a large Asian man who stood about six feet two inches tall and weighed approximately 350 pounds. The woman nodded and walked away.

The large man opened the door and said in perfect English, "Y'all can go in."

Cindy walked into the room first with Vega and Butcher following closely behind her. The large room was lit in red florescent lights. Chinese artwork and writing covered the walls. A short Asian man was seated at the only booth inside the room. He was surrounded by three large men, all bigger than the one who guarded the door. A few feet away another Asian man sat at an all-white grand piano playing classical music. When they approached the table, Cindy leaned down and kissed her older brother on both of his cheeks. After they exchanged a few words in Chinese, Cindy turned to Vega and said, "Just be straight up. I'll be inside the truck waiting."

Then she leaned up and kissed Vega on the lips. When Bobby saw his sister kiss Vega, he didn't show any emotion at all. Neither did any of his huge, hard-faced bodyguards.

After Cindy walked out of the room, Bobby said, "Y'all can both sit down."

Vega and Butcher both nervously sat down inside the booth. Bobby Chang was a forty-year-old man who stood only five feet five inches tall. He had a light brown complexion and dark black hair that was gathered into a ponytail that hung down his back. Both Vega and Butcher knew that they were in the presence of a very powerful man. It was well known throughout Philly, New Jersey, and New York that Bobby Chang's Asian Mafia Family had caused lots of casualties to their rivals—the East Coast Russian mob—with their well publicized drugs, guns, and illegal diamond wars.

"My sister has told me many good things about you, Vega," Bobby said, looking straight into his eyes.

Vega smiled and nodded.

"I have two brothers," Bobby continued. "Cindy's the only girl."

"She's a good girl," Vega said.

"First of all, let me get one thing straight. Cindy is a twenty-seven-year-old grown woman. What she does with her life is her own business. My family doesn't interfere, but like I said, she's the only girl, and I love her dearly."

Vega looked at Bobby and saw the seriousness in his dark brown eyes. He understood exactly what Bobby was saying: Take care of my little sister, and protect her like your life depended on it, or else deal with me.

"I understood, Mr. Chang," Vega replied.

"Good, now you can call me Bobby, and let's get down to the real reason we're all here."

Butcher finally relaxed and a smile came to his face.

"I need a new connect, Bobby, and I think you can be the man I'm in need of," Vega said.

"What is it you're looking for?" Bobby asked as he crossed his arms.

"Cocaine."

"How much cocaine are you talking about?"

"Two hundred kilos," Vega said.

"And how much do you have to spend?"

"Whatever the cost!" Vega said proudly.

Bobby nodded.

"Well in that case, how about I sell you two hundred kilos, and front you another two hundred kilos?"

"What's your price?"

"Fourteen thousand a key."

"Just tell me the place and time," Vega said.

"Slow down, Vega. It's not that simple. In every game there are many rules and penalties."

"And they are?"

"What you take is all yours. I don't want any excuses. Just my money. And as you well know, dealing with authorities is prohibited."

"We ain't no snitches!" Butcher said.

Bobby shot a quick glance at Butcher and said, "For y'all sakes, and everyone you love, I truly hope not."

"You don't have to worry about that, Bobby," Vega said confidently. "I and all my men can hold our tongues and play the hand that is dealt to us."

"There is one other thing that really bothers me," Bobby said as he stood.

"What's that?" Vega asked as he and Butcher also stood.

"The war with Underworld. He's a very powerful man, Vega. And he's connected to very powerful people. There are major consequences in going up against Underworld. He is the reason why my cocaine business has been taking major losses the last few years. I don't like him personally, but I can't help but respect the man. I heard about his parents' deaths, and the assassination attempt on his fiancée. If that was your work, I hope you're prepared for the ultimate battle."

"I'm prepared," Vega said.

"Just remember, my little sister is your responsibility," Bobby reminded him.

"She's in good hands."

"OK, then, I'll have someone call you in a few days and we'll take it from there."

After they shook hands, Vega and Butcher walked over to the door. Before they walked out, Bobby said, "Good luck."

While Junie drove, Vega and Cindy were locked in a passionate kiss. Butcher sat up front in the passenger seat, smiling from ear to ear.

"Is everything good now, daddy?" Cindy asked as she reached her hand down inside his pants.

"Everything is wonderful," Vega answered.

"My brother is a real serious guy. If you do him right, he will do you right," Cindy said as she rubbed up and down Vega's hard manhood.

"Don't worry, beautiful. I'm gonna do him right. He's the plug I've been waiting for, and now because of you, I'm gonna make a whole lot of money."

Junie turned the truck onto Market Street and headed toward the house in Southwest Philly. While Butcher was talking to someone on his cell phone, Vega and Cindy continued their conversation.

"So, daddy, what's up for tonight?" Cindy asked, kissing Vega softly around the neck.

"You know the rules. Sundays are for the wife and child."

"Come on, daddy, just this one time. I promise that me and Jewell will take it easy on you."

"Cindy, I promise you that tomorrow you and Jewell will get all of my undivided attention. I'll be over at the house early in the morning," Vega said as he sat back enjoying her soft hands caressing his dick. Cindy pouted like a spoiled little child. Vega leaned forward, kissed her on the lips, and said, "You and Jewell should rest up today, because tomorrow y'all gonna need it."

After Graveyard had a brief meeting with eight of Frank's top men and the three women of DNA, they all left his hotel room and went their separate ways. Graveyard was confident that everyone knew their upcoming jobs. The plan was now set and ready to go into full motion. All they needed now was word from Frank to begin their deadly assault.

Graveyard drove by the Dollhouse and spotted the big giant standing by the Jeep Cherokee smoking a blunt. *Once again it is perfect timing,* he thought, but he had to wait for Frank to tell him it was time to begin. Instead, Graveyard decided to check on all the other properties on Vega's list. Then afterward he would head straight to the cemetery.

Hahnemann University Hospital

Cassie stood in the doorway with tears streaming down her face. Seeing Valerie there with IVs in her arms, tubes inside her nose and mouth, and her face all bandaged was one of the worst sights she had ever seen. Riley, J-Dawg, and Valerie's family were all standing around inside the room. After Cassie said a silent prayer, she turned and walked away. Riley and J-Dawg followed right behind her.

When Cassie walked out of the hospital, two large men dressed in all black were waiting for her. Both men were armed and ready to shoot on sight. As they stood around waiting, a tinted black limousine pulled up and parked. The back door quickly swung open. Cassie, Riley, and J-Dawg all climbed into the back of the limo where another bodyguard was waiting inside. Then the limo drove off, and two men on motorcycles pulled up beside it. It was their job to make sure that everyone inside the limo got home safely.

CHAPTER 24

Miami
The Bentley Hotel, South Beach

CRAIG WAITED IN THE LUXURIOUS lobby of the Bentley Hotel while Frank went up to the penthouse suite to talk with Mr. Sanchez. Their trip to Miami was very unexpected. But Frank and Craig knew that whenever Mr. Sanchez called, you dropped what you were doing and hurried to meet him.

Upstairs inside the luxurious penthouse suite, Frank sat on the soft leather sofa waiting for Mr. Sanchez to finally appear. Two very attractive women sat over at a small table talking in Spanish. Frank couldn't understand a word being said. Both of the women were tall with model-worthy bodies and long, silky hair hanging down their backs. Every so often Frank would catch them looking over and smiling at him. Even though he didn't understand Spanish, he was sure that he was the main focus of their conversation.

Dressed in a long, white silk robe, Mr. Sanchez finally appeared from the bedroom. "Ladies, leave us," he ordered.

Both women stood from the table and walked away. Frank let his eyes follow them out of the room.

"I've seen those two women before," Frank said.

"One was Ms. Universe two years ago, and the other was Ms. Columbia last year. They're both good friends of mine," Mr. Sanchez said as he sat back on the sofa and got comfortable. "Frank, I needed to talk to you face to face."

"About what?"

"About what's going on in Philadelphia. Your face and company have been all over the news. That's not good at all for men in our business."

"I'm sorry, Mr. Sanchez, but a few of these things I had no control over. I and my boys are on it as we speak."

"I hope so. There is too much negative attention going your way. And I don't want no nosey investigative reporters finding out things that they shouldn't know. Who is this street punk, Vega?"

"How do you know about Vega?" Frank asked, shocked.

"I have my own sources down in Philly to keep me posted on all that I need to know. Now once again who is this punk that's been giving you a shitload of problems?"

"He's nobody, Mr. Sanchez, and right now he and everyone in his crew are all dead men walking! Vega is some wannabe gangster who wants my spot, a spot that he can't handle nor one that he will ever get."

"Is he the man responsible for your parents' deaths, the murder of the church deacon, and the assassination attempt on your fiancée?"

"Yes, Mr. Sanchez, he's the man behind everything," Frank answered, becoming more suspicious about where Mr. Sanchez was receiving his information.

Mr. Sanchez looked Frank straight in the eyes. After a long sigh he said, "There is a quote that I once read by a man named J. Glenn Gray. He said, „When two powers make war against each other, the anger and hatred that arise can be appeased only by the death of one or the other.' Do you understand that?"

"Yes, and I can assure you, Mr. Sanchez, that Vega will be the one who dies."

"I believe you, Frank. All I'm sayin' is do it fast before this thing gets way out of hand. You are a major player in my organization, and a very good friend also. I'm sure you've been working on a plan to get this Vega guy out of the way. Just do it soon and discretely is all I ask of you."

"You got my word, Mr. Sanchez. Like I said, Vega and his whole crew are already dead! They just don't know it yet," Frank said as he stood.

When Mr. Sanchez stood, they shook hands and he walked Frank over to the door.

"Girls, y'all can come back in now," Mr. Sanchez yelled out.

With smiles on their faces, both women walked into the living room and sat back down at the small table.

"I think Ms. Universe likes Frank," Mr. Sanchez said with a grin. "Would you like to stay a while and get to know her better? There's a private room in the back."

Frank looked over at the two gorgeous women and just shook his head. Even though the offer was very tempting, he couldn't do it.

"I'm sorry, Mr. Sanchez, but I have my own Ms. Universe back at home," he said.

After they shook hands again, Frank waved goodbye to the two smiling beauties and walked out of the suite. When he walked off the elevator and into the quiet lobby, Craig quickly spotted him and walked over to meet Frank.

"What's up?" Craig asked. "What did Mr. Sanchez want to talk about?"

"Vega," Frank said as they walked out of the hotel.

"Vega! How does he know about Vega?"

"I don't know, Craig, but he knows about him, and he's very concerned about what's going on in Philly," Frank said as they both got inside the back of the waiting limousine.

The limo pulled off and headed back to the airport.

"So what did he say about it?" Craig asked.

"He told me to fix the problem, and fix it fast, because there's already too much negative attention surrounding this shit!"

"Well everybody's ready. We're just waiting for you to give us the word."

"Tuesday is the day."

"Why Tuesday?"

"Because Tuesday is the day of the rap concert. While Vega and his crew are being wiped out, me and you will be back stage at the show taking pictures with celebrities."

"So you're gonna use the rap concert as our alibi?" Craig asked with a smile.

"That's right, my friend. It's the perfect alibi. And while we're inside enjoying ourselves, Graveyard will be outside earning his money."

City Line Avenue

Raquel and Vega watched Erika and two of her closest friends play inside the small pool out back. Vega had his arms wrapped around Raquel's plump stomach. Sundays were always family days, the only day of the week that Vega didn't go by his house in Southwest Philly.

"How did your meeting go this morning?" Raquel asked as she enjoyed his strong hands rubbing her stomach.

"The meeting went very well," Vega said and smiled.

As they stood there watching the children splashing water on each other, Vega couldn't help but feel like the happiest man alive. This was the life he had always wanted, and once Underworld was dead, his life would be complete.

Later that night

When Frank walked back into the house, Cassie was sitting on the sofa talking on her cell phone. Instant relief filled her at the sight of him returning in one piece.

"Riley, Frank just walked through the door. I'ma see you at the meeting tomorrow," she said and then closed her cell phone and laid it beside her.

Frank took off his jacket, walked over to Cassie, and sat down beside her. They leaned forward and gave each other a kiss and hug.

"How did everything turn out?" she asked, looking into Frank's serious brown eyes.

"Everything went well. Nothing to worry about," Frank said. "Tuesday me and Craig will be at the concert with you."

Cassie's eyes widened with shock. Frank hardly ever went to one of the rap shows. He tried his best to stay low key and as far away from the public eye as he could.

"I'll be hanging around backstage with you," he said.

Cassie knew Frank better than anyone else. So she knew that there was more to it. Everything that Frank did was meticulously planned out.

"Keeping an eye on your girl, huh?" Cassie asked as she laid her head across his lap.

"Yeah, and our unborn child," he said as he leaned down and softly kissed her on the lips.

***

Inside the empty cemetery, Graveyard stood a few feet away from three, ten-feet deep holes. He was surrounded by hundreds of tombstones. Graveyard let out a long sigh, stretching his arms high above his head. Ever since he was a young child growing up on the mean streets of Cleveland, there had been something about graveyards that interested him. Throughout his life he had sent many people to the dark world of death.

After walking around the three large holes, Graveyard turned and walked away, smiling at the knowledge that the three empty graves would soon be filled.

Chapter 25

Monday afternoon

INSIDE THE LARGE CONFERENCE ROOM, Cassie sat at the head of the long oval table conducting a meeting with her top staff members. A few of the label's new artists were also present.

"The show will start at seven thirty," Cassie said. "I want all of our artists that are performing to be there at six to go over their stage performances. Did you get that, J-Dawg?" Cassie asked and everyone started laughing.

"Yeah, I get it, Cassie. Don't worry, I'll be there," J-Dawg responded.

"In what spot will J-Dawg be performing?" Riley asked.

"He'll be fourth, right before the main performance goes on stage," Cassie said as she looked around the table.

Cassie looked over at the group of young men who stood quietly over in the corner. They were the members of ICH (Inner City Hustlers), a new rap group that she had recently signed to the label.

"ICH, y'all will be the opening act," Cassie said.

After the meeting ended, Cassie was escorted out of a back door by two of Frank's men. When she walked out the door, a tinted black Mercedes Benz was waiting for her. A man in dark shades sat behind the wheel. Cassie climbed into the backseat and closed the door.

"Where to?" he asked.

"Take me back to the hospital," Cassie said as she took out her cell phone and started making calls.

When the car pulled off, two bodyguards on their Kawasaki motorcycles followed right behind them.

Inside their unmarked car, Agents Mitchell and Stokes were parked right across the street from Underworld Entertainment.

"Wednesday we're sending one of our paid street informants into the club," Mitchell said. "So far that's our best bet if we plan to get to Vega and his crew. And that's the only way to get to Frank, it seems. Frank's operation seems flawless. We don't have nothing on the guy but a few statements from our jailhouse informants."

"But they are supposed to give their statements to the grand jury later that week," Stokes said.

"We still need more to bring down Frank!" Mitchell vented.

"So you think that the best way to get to Frank is through getting to Vega first?"

"I believe that's what it will take. If that don't work, I'll ask the FBI director to put together a multi agency force with the FBI, DEA, and Homeland Security to take down Frank's ass!"

Southwest Philly

Vega stood in front of everyone holding three pieces of white paper. Junie sat back smiling. He was the only person in the room who knew what the papers said. Butcher and Homicide stood along the wall while Artie was seated on the sofa next to Spade and Canon. Cindy and Jewell stood together by the large plasma TV.

"These three pieces of paper in my hand contain some very important information that I found out three years ago. After gathering this information, I began putting my plan together to bring down Frank „Underworld' Simms! Then when my brother Tony was kidnapped and beheaded, that only added more fuel to my already burning fire. But these three pieces of paper in my hand are the main reason why I want to destroy Frank and everyone he loves."

"What do the papers say?" Butcher asked.

"After Frank is dead I will reveal to all of you what's on these papers. Then everyone inside this room will understand my hatred toward Frank Simms. The contract on Frank's head has now been raised to two hundred fifty thousand dollars, and one hundred fifty thousand for Craig and Cassie." Everyone's faces lit up with excitement at that news.

"Tomorrow night is the rap concert at the Civic Center," Vega continued. "I'm sure they'll all be there. Everyone has guns, hats, jerseys, and walkie-talkies. Tomorrow night I'll be here alone with my two girls. Y'all have a key and the emergency number to my private phone. So call me and keep me up to date on what's going on. After the show is over I want everyone in this room to meet back here," Vega said as he rolled up the three pieces of paper and put them inside his jacket pocket. Then he turned and walked toward the stairs with Cindy and Jewell following closely behind.

While Artie drove down Chester Avenue, his mind was clouded with thoughts of Frank and the money he could make if he succeeded in killing him. He knew that Frank and all of his loved ones would be protected by bodyguards. If he had to kill them all just to get to Frank, he would do just that. Artie already planned on using his police badge to his advantage. There were a lot of privileges that came with being a police detective, and getting access to enter certain venues was one of the main privileges.

Downtown Philly

A black limousine pulled up in front of the federal courthouse building. Robert Steiner quickly opened the back door and got inside. Frank and Craig both sat inside, waiting. The limo slowly pulled off into the congested streets of downtown Philly.

Robert had no idea why Frank wanted to see him. Even though he was due for trial in two more hours, he knew not to keep Frank Simms waiting. The limo turned down Market Street and onto Broad Street.

"Frank, what is the urgency?" Robert asked after noticing the serious expressions on both men's faces.

"How do you know Mr. Sanchez?" Frank asked.

Robert's startled eyes opened wide. "How did . . . how . . ."

"Never mind how I found out, Robert. Just tell me how you know him. And why have you been telling him all of my business?"

"Frank, I met Mr. Sanchez a few months ago at a corporate business owners' seminar in New York. I represented a few wealthy clients who were there. Anyway, me and Mr. Sanchez were introduced by a mutual friend. After I told him I lived in Philadelphia and had my own law firm we started talking. That was when your name came up in the conversation."

"So then what happened?" Frank asked.

"Mr. Sanchez told me that you were a very good friend of his, and to do whatever I could to keep you out of trouble," Robert said nervously.

Frank and Craig smiled.

"Mr. Sanchez gave me a private phone number to reach him so I could keep him up to date on all that was going on with you in Philadelphia. A few days ago I called him and told Mr. Sanchez about this guy Vega. The conversation was brief."

"So how do you benefit from this?" Craig asked.

"Power! Money has nothing to do with this. In the real game of life, it's what you know and who you know. A favor for a favor," Robert said.

Even though Frank didn't appreciate being spied on by his own lawyer, he understood why Robert did it.

"Frank, Mr. Sanchez likes you a lot. He's only concerned about your well-being. And as we all know, he has a lot invested in you."

Frank looked deep into Robert's blue eyes and said, "Just do me a favor and never tell him another thing about me."

"You got my word on it, Frank." Robert said as they shook hands. "How did you find out?" he asked.

"I saw Mr. Sanchez yesterday in Miami. When he mentioned the name Vega, I knew that there was only one person who could've told him about what was going on in Philly. You."

When the limousine pulled back up in front of the Federal Courthouse Robert got out and closed the door. Then the limousine slowly drove away.

Chapter 26

One hour later

ASSISTANT DISTRICT ATTORNEY PETE CHILDS stood on a street near Rittenhouse Square. When the tinted black limousine pulled up in front of him, Pete quickly opened the door and got inside.

"Frank, what the hell is going on!" Pete asked.

"You tell me," Frank said in a calm tone.

"First your parents get murdered, then the Deacon gets killed at the same church, and now someone tries to kill Cassie in a drive-by," Pete said with concern written all over his face.

"Pete, calm down. All of this will be straightened out very soon," Frank said.

"Frank, that's not all, my friend. Yesterday Vega was seen by one of my men down in Chinatown."

"Chinatown! For what?"

"I think he's planning on doing some street business with Bobby Chang, the boss of the Asian Mafia Family."

Frank looked over at Craig and they both shook their heads in total disbelief.

"You know just as well as I do that if those two lunatics get together, we'll have a whole lot of shit on our hands!" Pete said. "Another thing I found out through my friends down at internal affairs is that Vega has a Philadelphia detective on his payroll, a guy by the name of Artie Fletcher."

"That must've been the guy that Graveyard spotted sitting outside the church in a parked car the day of my parents' funeral," Frank said.

"Frank, you have to fix this problem or the DA's office will be coming to fix it for you. You don't need them snooping around. Neither of us do! If they ever find out that I'm your inside source, I'll be fired and sent straight to federal prison."

"Don't worry, Pete. I would never let that happen," Frank said with confidence.

"I know you won't, Frank. I've been working for you for too many years, but it's never been this bad before. In fact, I've never seen someone got at you as hard as Vega. And I'm surprised that he's still alive," Pete said in a serious tone.

"Pete, I said I'll take care of everything. Now just trust me, my friend," Frank replied.

"What's up with the feds?" Craig asked.

"They're still investigating y'all and Vega's crew. So far they ain't got nothing. But they can get pissed off and call in for more reinforcements to help get this investigation really off the ground. You know how the feds play—always by their own rules."

Frank sat there in total silence. His mind was now racing with thoughts. Finally Frank looked over at Pete and said, "Do your sons like rap music?"

"Huh? Yeah, I'm sure they do. What teenage boys don't?"

"Tomorrow I would like to invite you and your two sons to the rap concert down at the Civic Center. Please don't ask any questions, Pete. Just say whether you can be there."

"Yeah, I don't see why not."

"Good. I'll pick y'all up in a limo and y'all can all hang backstage with me and the celebrities," Frank said as he and Craig looked at each other and smiled. Pete just sat there shaking his head, wondering what was going on inside Frank's mind.

Later that night
Outside the Dollhouse Gentlemen's Club

"Look here, Homicide, once we start dealing with Bobby Chang, we will become unstoppable!" Butcher said with excitement.
"With his muscle behind us, we can't lose!" Homicide said, grinning from ear to ear.
"Once Underworld is dead and gone, Philly is ours! And ain't nothing or nobody who can do anything about it," Butcher said as he passed the blunt he held to Homicide.
Homicide took a long pull, then blew the thick cloud of smoke out through his nose. "I feel you, homie. You know me. I'm down all the way,"
"Damn, I still can't believe that little Chinese whore Cindy is Bobby Chang's lil sister," Butcher said.
"Small world, huh?" Homicide asked, passing back the blunt. "So what do you think is on those papers that Vega had?"
"I'm not really sure, but I do know this. A few years ago Vega hired a private investigator to find out some important things, but he never told me what they were," Butcher said, blowing out a thick cloud of smoke.
"Do you think he found out something on Underworld?"
"Yeah, he had to. That's why Vega hates the man so much. Whatever it is that Vega found out, he took it very personally," Butcher said.
"Well when Frank is dead, we'll all find out," Homicide replied as they both started laughing.

Standing almost a block away, Graveyard was looking through his night vision binoculars, watching both men closely. He was itching to just walk by and kill them both. But Frank had already laid out the plan. A fast death would be the easy way out. Frank wanted Vega and his people to feel every inch of his wrath. Slow torture and then death were what Frank had ordered.

Graveyard had spotted the two FBI agents sitting inside their unmarked car. They were also watching the two men outside the Dollhouse. It all now made sense. The two agents were investigating Vega's crew and Frank's crew, hoping to gather enough information to come down with a shitload of federal indictments. But their time was limited too. Vega wasn't Frank's only enemy. So was any law enforcement agency that tried to take down Frank. And they would all feel his wrath.

From the last few days of watching and scoping out the scene, Graveyard had learned everything he needed to know to capture and destroy the enemy. This was a war, a war of the streets. And the streets were a place where only the strongest, smartest and most powerful people survived.

After Graveyard put away his binoculars and got back into his car, he pulled off down the dark, quiet street. Tuesday couldn't come fast enough for him. Ever since coming to Philly, kill day had been the one day for which he was yearning.

Craig stood out on the balcony of his condominium looking out into the dark beautiful city that surrounded him. As he stood there, a cool wind brushed against his body. Every night before he turned in to bed, he would come out on the balcony and enjoy the tranquility of the night. This was where Craig would let his mind become totally free and escape all the madness of the world.

On this night Craig thought about just how fortunate he really was. Altogether the legal and illegal aspects of Underworld organization were making over five million dollars each month. And their attorney had set them up with offshore accounts in the Cayman Islands to hide most of their illegal drug profits. Frank and Craig had also invested their money into some of the new casinos that were being built in Canada and all throughout the Caribbean islands.

Craig smiled, knowing that he was living the life that so many others had only dreamed of—the plush condominium, S-600 Benz, and his secret affair with the beautiful Janell Jones, one of the most successful recording artists in the whole world.

My life is good, Craig thought as the cool midnight breeze continued to brush against his skin. Craig opened his silk Gucci robe and raised his arms high above his head. For a moment he just stood there inhaling the midnight air. *This is the life,* he thought. *The only life I ever wanted to live.* And Craig would have no problem killing anyone who tried to take it away.

While Cassie was in bed sleeping soundly, Frank eased out of bed and tiptoed out of the bedroom. He couldn't sleep because there were just too many things going through his mind. He walked downstairs and over to a picture that was hanging on the wall. He stood there staring at an old picture of him and his two smiling parents when Frank just was ten-years-old. He was their only child, and together they gave Frank the world. Frank still couldn't believe that they were both gone, dead because of the wrath of his most hated enemy.

As Frank stood there staring hard into the picture, a lonely tear fell from the corner of his left eye and slowly rolled down the side of his face. When Frank turned around to return upstairs, he saw Cassie standing a few feet away, watching him.

She walked up to Frank and grabbed his hand. "Come on, baby, let's go back to bed," she said.

Frank looked at the picture once more before he turned away. Then he followed his beautiful fiancée back upstairs. When they got in bed they cuddled until they both fell asleep in each other's arms.

Chapter 27

Tuesday afternoon

THE PLAN TO TAKE DOWN Vega and his whole crew was set and already in motion. Frank had black tinted vans with three of his top men in each one situated all around the city. Wherever Vega owned a piece of property, one of the vans was parked close by with men inside, watching and patiently waiting for the right time to strike. Neither Vega nor anyone else in his organization knew that the war Vega had declared on Underworld was about to become the biggest mistake he had ever made.

When Homicide pulled up in front of the Dollhouse Gentlemen's Club, the three men inside the black van were all watching very closely. Each man held a loaded 9 mm pistol with an attached silencer. As soon as Homicide got out of his car, the van sped up beside him and the two doors quickly slid open. Before Homicide could run or reach for his weapon, the men had their guns pointed at his unprotected head.

"Try anything and you will die right here!" Graveyard said. "Now get the fuck in the van!"

Homicide knew that he had no other choice but to obey the man's orders. As soon as he climbed into the van, the door slid closed and the van sped off. Homicide was quickly handcuffed and pushed down to his knees. Fear was written all over his face. He still had no idea who the men were. But what he did know was that they weren't cops.

"Please, man! Please! What is it y'all want?" Graveyard asked.

"Shut the fuck up, you big coward, and don't say one word!" Graveyard yelled.

Smack! Graveyard hit Homicide as hard as he could with his pistol, knocking the six-foot-seven giant out cold. He then went into Homicide's pockets and took out everything inside—keys, a walkie-talkie, and a stack of hundred-dollar bills.

Thirty minutes later the van drove into Frank's gated warehouse in Yeadon. Homicide was just coming to after receiving the hard blow to the side of his head. Once the van was safely inside the warehouse, the doors slid open and Homicide was pushed onto the ground. Two more men stood around him, both dressed in black and pointing their guns at his head. All three men got out of the van and walked over to where Homicide lay on the ground.

"Please, man!" Homicide begged. "I'll tell y'all whatever you need to know!

"You say another word, and I'ma shoot you right between your fucking eyes!" Graveyard said as he took out his cell phone and dialed a number.

"Underworld, we got the first one," he said into the phone. When Homicide heard the name Underworld, he couldn't believe it. As he lay there on the ground shaking his head, he knew he had fucked up. Big time.

Hahnemann University Hospital

Cassie and Riley stood on the side of Valerie's hospital bed, holding her hands. They had been there all morning. Three days after being shot, Valerie was now coherent and able to move and say a few words. The bullet that hit her face went straight through her mouth, leaving only minimal damage. Cassie stood there with tears streaming from her eyes, feeling totally responsible for what had happened to her friend. For three days they had prayed non-stop. And now their prayers had finally paid off.

"Do you feel OK?" Cassie asked.

Valerie nodded.

"Val, I'm sorry," Cassie said, unable to hold it back any longer. Val squeezed her hand as hard as she could. Then the tears started falling from her eyes.

"Don't be," she said in a soft voice.

Cassie leaned down and kissed her friend on the lips.

"I'll try," she said as they both smiled.

After Cassie and Riley left the hospital, they got back inside the secured limousine and were driven back to the company. Both of them felt the best that they had felt in the last three days. Valerie was going to be all right.

Inside the FBI office in downtown Philadelphia, Agent Mitchell and his partner Stokes were inside a small office talking.

"What time do you want to drive by and check things out?" Stokes asked as he took a seat in the empty chair.

"I have a lot of paperwork to do. Maybe later we can swing by Frank's entertainment company and see what we can find. I already got our informant ready to go check out the Dollhouse tomorrow night. So sooner or later we'll have someone get into Vega's circle and help us bring him down," Mitchell said as he sat down at his desk and took a sip of his coffee.

"That's fine with me. We'll just park in our quiet little spot and wait and see what happens," Stokes said.

"All you want to do is watch those little whores who be walking up and down the street," Mitchell said and laughed.

"Don't try to blame it all on me. I see you peeping at them also," Stokes said jokingly. When Mitchell took out a white piece of paper, Stokes asked, "What's that?"

"Oh, I've put together a list of the top drug bosses from around the city. We got Frank „Underworld' Simms, Bobby Chang, the boss of the AMF, Vega Littles, Kevin „Meatloaf' Sanders, Lloyd „Domino' Jeffries, James „Bingo' Roberts, and the only female, Tanya „Passion' Pitts. I scratched off Carlos Benitez, the boss of the Dominican cartel after he was murdered last week."

"Wow, that's one helluva list," Stokes said.

"Yeah, but the crazy part about it is everyone on the list except Bobby Chang and Vega Littles works for Frank. At least that's what the jailhouse informants told us," Mitchell said, sipping on his coffee.

"Think they're telling us the truth?" Stokes asked.

"Who knows. Only time will tell," Mitchell said.

An hour later

Homicide lay on the ground, handcuffed with a blindfold covering his eyes. All he could hear was the sound of footsteps walking around him. He was more scared than he had ever been in his life. Suddenly the footsteps stopped. When the blindfold was removed, he couldn't believe who was now standing right in front of him. Dressed in a black Italian designer suit and a pair of black alligator shoes was none other than Frank "Underworld" Simms, looking like he had just stepped out of the pages of *GQ* magazine. Standing by his side was his right hand man, Craig, who was also dressed in a black suit and a matching pair of alligator shoes.

Graveyard and the other men all stood around looking at their large human prey. Frank looked into Homicide's scared eyes and asked, "Who killed my parents?"

"Vega sent Spade and Canon to do it," Homicide said immediately.

"Are those the two people who live in Vega's row house on Forty-third Street?"

"Yeah . . . uh . . . ha . . ." Homicide said, shocked that Underworld knew so much.

"So Spade is a girl?" Frank asked.

Homicide nodded.

"Who killed the deacon?" Frank asked calmly.

"Spade and Canon did that too," Homicide said without any hesitation. "They're Vega's top two killers, because no one expects them to be so ruthless."

"Now tell me, who was it that tried to kill my fiancée, Cassie?"

"That was Artie. He's a detective who works for Vega. He set that up all by himself, and . . ."

"And what?" Frank asked, feeling the rage inside him starting to boil.

"And he wanted the money that Vega put on your head," Homicide mumbled.

"How much did he put on my head?"

"Two hundred fifty grand, and one fifty on Cassie and your partner Craig. Please, I'll tell you whatever you want. Just don't kill me. I got two kids and—"

"Tiffany, seven, and your three-year-old son Ryan Jr.," Frank said, cutting off Homicide.

Homicide couldn't believe his ears. Frank knew everything about him.

Frank leaned down and grabbed Homicide by the collar.

"Please, Underworld!" Homicide begged. "Please, I'll tell you everything!"

"I already know about the house in Southwest Philly where Vega is right now! Him and those two whores!" Frank said. "Do you know who the fuck I am? Do you?"

"Yes . . . yes! You're Underworld!" Homicide said, trembling.

"What does Vega have planned that I am not aware of?"

"He's gonna have everyone out at the rap concert tonight."

"For what?"

"To try to kill you, Craig, or Cassie. We're all supposed to wear our red Phillies caps and jerseys tonight so we'll know who's who. Vega gave us all walkie-talkies to communicate. Me, Spade, Canon, Butcher, Junie, and Artie," Homicide said, spilling his guts.

"So that's what he's got planned?" Frank asked as he looked around at everybody. "What else you ain't telling me?"

"He got some white papers that he's gonna show us."

"Papers? What are you talking about?" Frank asked.

"I don't know what the papers are, but he said what's on the three pieces of paper is the reason why he hates you so much. He hates you more than he does snakes."

"Snakes?"

"Yeah, snakes. Vega can't stand the sight of them."

Frank called one of his men over and pulled him to the side. After whispering something into his ear, the man said, "Don't worry. I'll take care of it, boss," and then he rushed away.

Homicide looked around at all the men who stood around him. He noticed that each one of them was wearing all black. They looked as if they were all going to a funeral. Then it hit him hard upside the head. They were.

"Please, Underworld! Please don't kill my two kids!" Homicide begged. "It was Vega's idea to kill your parents! I swear it was!" Homicide said as he crawled on his knees toward Frank.

Smack! Everyone watched as Homicide's huge body slumped to the ground. Graveyard had hit Homicide in the back of his head with his pistol, knocking him out cold again. After one of the men wrapped duct tape around his mouth and placed the blindfold back over his eyes, the other men helped pick up Homicide and carry him back into the van.

"Graveyard, you know what to do next," Frank said. "Around seven start grabbing all of their asses! Save Vega for last, and make sure you destroy every piece of property he owns. I'll see you immediately after the show is over," Frank said as he and Craig turned and walked away. Graveyard and two of the men climbed into the van and closed the sliding door. After they waited ten minutes, they started the van and drove out of the warehouse, headed for the cemetery and the three freshly dug ten-foot graves.

Underworld Entertainment, 5:48 PM

The elevator swung open and Cassie, Riley, and J-Dawg all stepped off into the ground floor garage. Two black limousines were parked a few feet away with four of Frank's top men guarding them. One of the limousines was for the label's artists. The other limo had been reserved for Cassie, Riley, and their top recording artist, J-Dawg.

When they had all climbed inside the limo, one of the men closed the door behind them. Then both limos slowly pulled off and drove out of the garage. When the limos pulled into the street, there were four men on motorcycles waiting for them. As the drivers headed toward the Philadelphia Civic Center, Cassie felt her two-way vibrating on her hip. She checked the text message and a smile came to her face. MISS YOU, SEE YOU IN AN HOUR. LOVE, FRANK.

Chapter 28

Northeast Philadelphia

THE LIMOUSINE PULLED UP IN front of Pete Childs's beautiful two-story home at six seventeen PM. Pete and his two teenage sons were standing outside eagerly waiting. When the limo door swung open, all three of them walked over and climbed inside. Then the limousine drove away, headed for the Philadelphia Civic Center. While the two boys sat back playing Xbox, Pete scooted over and put his mouth to Frank's ear.

"Frank, I don't know what's going on, but I know you got something up your Armani sleeves," he whispered.

"Everything I do has a reason behind it, Pete, and you out of anybody should know that. But for now just sit back and enjoy the ride, my friend," Frank said softly.

Pete sat back and relaxed. He looked over at Craig who was talking to Janell on his cell phone. Then he looked over at his two excited teenage sons. When he glanced back over at Frank, Frank was sitting back with a big smile on his face, looking like a man without a problem or care in the world.

Forty minutes later the limousine arrived at the Civic Center and entered the private celebrity parking lot. Everyone got out and was quickly escorted inside by the Civic Center Security team. After going through a series of doors and a long hallway, they were finally backstage. The private backstage area was filled with celebrities, managers, music reporters, and photographers. All the top people in the Philly music scene were there.

Singer Musiq Soulchild was talking to Jill Scott. Eve was laughing with the guys from ICH, and rapper Beanie Sigel was engaged in a heated conversation with members of the Roots. Representatives from all the major urban magazines—*The Source*, *Ozone*, *XXL*, *Vibe*, *King*, and *Smooth*—were also present. And the local video show, *Urban Expressions*, was preparing to record the entire show.

Frank walked around with Pete and his two excited sons, introducing them to all of his celebrity friends. Pete's sons were two of J-Dawg's biggest fans, so Frank made sure they got a few exclusive pictures with J-Dawg. The entire backstage area was blocked off by a tight Civic Center security team, making everyone in the backstage area feel safe and secure. Picture phones were snapping, cell phones were ringing, and two-ways were vibrating out of control.

Craig slipped away into the crowd. Moments later he returned and whispered something into Frank's ear. Frank looked at his platinum and diamond Rolex and saw that the time was now four minutes after seven. With a big smile on his face, he walked over to Pete and Cassie and said, "Come on, let's take a few pictures together."

For the rest of the night, Frank was gonna keep Pete right by his side.

City Line Avenue, 7:09 PM

The three men inside the tinted black van had been waiting for the right moment to make their move. That time was now. As soon as Raquel and Erika pulled up inside the Lexus and parked, the doors to the van parked right behind them quickly slid open. As soon as Raquel and Erika got out of the car, two of the men rushed up on them, pointing loaded guns. The mother-daughter pair was grabbed quickly and thrown into the van. It all happened in less than two minutes on this quiet, suburban street, and no one saw a thing.

After the van sped off and disappeared around the corner, another tinted black van pulled up in front of Vega's beautiful house. A man dressed in all black quickly got out. Inside his hand was a U.S. issued Army hand grenade. Without hesitation he popped the pin and threw the grenade through the front window.

Booooommm! The loud explosion sounded like a meteor had crashed to the earth. The house caught fire instantly. Flames, smoke, and debris were everywhere. When the neighbors started coming out of their homes to see what all the noise and commotion was about, they couldn't believe their eyes. The once beautiful home was now engulfed in blazing flames. And the tinted black van was nowhere in sight.

At 7:13 PM Junie stood outside the Civic Center, observing the large crowd. Suddenly three beautiful women walked up to him.

"Excuse me," one of the women said. "We're having a problem with our car. It's parked right around the corner. Could you please come check it out for us?"

Junie looked at the three attractive young women and said, "Yeah, why not?"

He followed the women around the corner and noticed a green Mercedes parked there with the hood up. Another beautiful female was standing by the car. Junie was so blinded by all the attractive women that he never paid attention to the tinted black van that was parked right beside the Mercedes. As soon as Junie walked up to the car, the woman standing by the car pulled out her loaded 9 mm pistol and the doors to the van slid wide open.

"Get the fuck in the van or die, motherfucker!" Passion said, pointing her gun at his head. Junie had no other option. Without hesitation he climbed into the van where three of Frank's men were inside waiting. He was immediately thrown down and handcuffed. After Passion slammed down the hood, she and the other women all got inside the Mercedes. Moments later, she pulled off down the street. The tinted van waited for the Mercedes to disappear, and then it drove off in the opposite direction.

7:29 PM

When Artie appeared in his unmarked police car, he was spotted instantly. He drove up to the two security guards who were in charge of celebrity parking and the backstage entrance. Both men noticed the red Phillies hat and baseball jersey that he wore. They had been waiting for him.

"I'm a detective with the Philadelphia Police," he said, showing off his badge.

Both men carefully looked at his badge, nodding and shaking their heads.

"Looks good to me," one of them said.

"OK, you can park your car over by that black van, and then I'll escort you inside," the other security guard said.

Artie smiled as he rolled up his window and drove over to the empty parking space next to the tinted black van. As soon as he stepped out of his car, the doors to the van slid wide open. In less than two minutes, Artie was inside the van handcuffed and lying face down next to Junie. They both had duct tape over their mouths and blindfolds covering their scared eyes. Once Junie and Artie were secure, the van drove off.

West Philadelphia, Forty-third Street, 7:34 PM

"We're late," Spade said as she and Canon walked out their front door holding hands. Both of them were dressed in their red Phillies hats, baseball jerseys, blue jeans, and Air Nike sneakers. Underneath their shirts were loaded 9 mms and walkie-talkies. They had called Junie to pick them up, but he never answered his cell phone or returned their pages, so they decided to catch a cab.

As soon as the smiling couple got halfway down the block, the van's doors slid open. Before Spade and Canon could reach for their weapons, they were both tackled hard to the ground by three large men. A few neighborhood drug dealers were standing around watching.

After Spade and Canon were thrown inside the van and driven away, one of the young men looked at his friend and said, "Mark, I told you they were feds in that black van! This block is too hot. I'm outta here," he said as he picked up his bag of crack rocks that was hidden underneath a car.

His friend Mark stood there for a moment, scratching his head. "Hey, lil Rob, hold up," he said, running behind him.

As soon as the two guys ran off, another man entered the block dressed in all black.

Inside his hand was a live hand grenade. He calmly walked up to the small row house and looked around. After pulling the pin and tossing the grenade through the front window, he ran off down the street.

Booommm! When the neighbors rushed out of their homes to see what the loud explosion was, the man had already run through an alley. When he exited the alley on another street, the tinted black van was right there waiting for him. After he got inside, the van pulled off down the street.

Chapter 29

7:46 PM

INSIDE THE CROWDED PHILADELPHIA CIVIC Center, Pete and his sons were having the time of their lives. Even though Pete wasn't a big rap fan, he got caught up in the excitement of the show. He had never been around so many celebrities in his life. When Philly native Will Smith and his bodyguard Charlie Mack appeared backstage, Pete almost had a heart attack. He was a big fan of Will Smith. Smith and Nicolas Cage were his two favorite actors.

Frank saw the excitement in Pete's eyes and walked Pete and his sons over to meet the famous Hollywood superstar. Together they took a few pictures with their camera phones.

After Will and his bodyguard walked off, Frank put his arm around Pete's shoulders and asked, "Are you enjoying yourself?"

"Am I! I just met Will Smith!" he said.

Frank smiled and said, "Come on. There go a few of the singers from Boys II Men. Let me introduce you to them."

With smiling faces, and camera phone ready, Pete and his sons followed Frank and Craig throughout the backstage VIP crowd. When Cassie and Frank saw each other, they both winked. Then Cassie turned back around and watched as her newly signed rap group, ICH, performed for its young, screaming fans.

While Frank, Craig, Pete, and his two sons walked around, meeting and taking pictures with different celebrities, Vega's world of luxury was slowly crumbling. Almost every one of his properties had been blown up and destroyed by fire. His soul food restaurant, pool hall, hair salon, social club, rental properties, and every vehicle at his two used-car dealerships had been set on fire. Fire stations from all around the city were working non-stop to end the fires, but there would be nothing left to salvage from any of Vega Littles's possessions.

Behind the Civic Center

Butcher looked at his gold Movado watch and noticed that the time was seven fifty-nine.
"Damn, where is everybody?" he asked aloud.
Parked behind the Civic Center, Butcher sat on the hood of his red Lexus. For the last twenty minutes he had been waiting for someone to call him. He'd called everyone on their walkie-talkies, but no one answered. Then he had called Junie's and Artie's cell phones, but neither one picked up.
A blue and white police car appeared and slowly drove toward him. Butcher had left his pistol inside the car, so he had no worries. When the police car stopped in front of him, a feeling of nervousness entered his body. Butcher noticed that only one officer was inside the vehicle. Suddenly the black officer got out of the car with his gun pointed at Butcher's chest.
"Whoa!" Butcher said. "Officer, what's wrong?"
"I just got a report on my radio saying that a red Lexus was just stolen a few blocks from here."
"I ain't steal shit, officer. This is my car!" Butcher said.

"Well turn around and let me handcuff you. If you're the real owner of the vehicle, I'll let you go."

"Man, this shit is crazy!" Butcher said as he turned around with both arms behind his back. After the officer handcuffed Butcher, the officer put Butcher inside the back of the his patrol car and closed the door.

"Officer, the car is mine!" Butcher yelled. When the officer got behind the wheel of his patrol car and pulled off, Butcher knew that something wasn't right. "Hey, man, what the fuck is going on?" Butcher asked. "You ain't check shit!"

The officer remained silent.

"Man, what the fuck is going on! Whatchu want, some money, you crooked motherfucker?" Butcher shouted.

Officer Cooper pulled up and parked his car right next to the tinted black van. Then he turned around to Butcher and said, "No, I don't need your money. Underworld already paid me!"

Butcher's eyes opened wide with fear at hearing that. "Oh, shit!" he yelled.

"And don't you worry. All of your friends are at the cemetery waiting for you," Cooper said and laughed.

Suddenly the doors on the van slid wide open and two men dressed in all black quickly got out. The sky was now dark, and no one was around when they dragged Butcher into the waiting van. When the van pulled off, Butcher lay inside, handcuffed, duct taped, and blindfolded, just like everyone else had been before him.

Forty minutes later the van pulled into the large cemetery on Lehigh Avenue in North Philadelphia. The van proceeded to the back of the cemetery and parked next to seven similar vans. The van's doors slid open, and Butcher was pushed out of the van. The two men grabbed his arms and started dragging his body toward the freshly dug graves. When the blindfold was pulled from Butcher's face, he was shocked to see Passion, Bingo, Domino, and Meatloaf—Frank's four top drug bosses—standing before him . Right behind them were three ten-foot deep graves. Butcher watched as the four drug bosses moved out of the way so Butcher could be walked over to the first grave.

When Butcher saw Vega's wife and six-year-old daughter handcuffed and duct taped inside the grave, he almost fainted. They were tearfully looking up at him, helpless and scared to death. The two men then walked Butcher over to the middle grave. When he looked down inside, he shook his head in total disbelief and fear. Junie, Homicide, Artie, Spade, and Canon were all lying inside this grave, handcuffed and duct taped. Then one of the men pushed Butcher down into the same deep grave. He fell hard into the others. The two men turned and walked back toward the vans. It was now time to wait.

8:55 PM

Pete stood in the corner, talking into his cell phone with a look of total disbelief on his face. His two sons stood by a wall conversing with J-Dawg while Frank and Craig stood by the back door having a deep conversation. Frank had just received a call from Graveyard, the call he had been waiting for all night. After Pete got off his cell phone, he walked up to both men with a big smile on his face.

"What's up?" Frank asked.

"I just got off the phone with the district attorney. He said that around seven o'clock this evening some houses and commercial properties around the city were set on fire. Firefighters are now checking for any bodies that may have gotten trapped in the fire."

"So what?" Frank asked with a sly grin on his face. Pete looked into Frank's eyes said, "Every piece of property belonged to a Mr. Vega Littles. Y'all set me up!" Pete said in a low whisper.

"Naw, we would never do that," Craig said and laughed.

"It's already done," Pete said. "All evening long y'all two have been here with me. I'm your alibi just in case anything ever went wrong. The assistant district attorney—the perfect alibi. I knew you were up to something, Frank," Pete said as he stood there shaking his head.

Frank put his arm around Pete's shoulders and said, "Pete, I don't know what you're talking about. I just wanted to invite my good friend and his two teenage sons out to a rap concert."

"Save it! You have pictures with us together, times, and so on. While we're in here smiling in celebrities' faces, Vega's whole empire is being destroyed. I see what's going on now." Pete looked at Frank and shook his head. "You had this planned all along. Now I see why you are the man you are. And to speak truthfully, I feel sorry for all your enemies."

Frank put his mouth to Pete's ear and whispered. "Don't be, because if they could, they would kill us both in a heartbeat."

Pete stood there frozen, knowing that every word Frank just said was the truth.

"Now, come on, Pete," Frank said. "Let's enjoy the rest of the show."

Southwest Philly, 9:16 PM

Graveyard used the key that he got from Homicide to enter the house. The downstairs was empty, but he could hear loud moans coming from an upstairs bedroom. Inside his hand was a pair of handcuffs and his loaded 9 mm with the attached silencer. He tiptoed up the stairs. When he reached the top of the stairs, the moans became louder. The smell of sex filled the air.

"Oh, yes, daddy! Yes! Yes!" a female voice screamed out.

Graveyard approached the bedroom door and slowly eased it open. When he looked inside he saw Vega lying on his back with an attractive Asian woman riding him like a cowgirl on a wild black stallion. Another naked woman—a tall, attractive blond—sat in a chair, sliding a ten-inch black dildo in and out of her pussy. Both women filled the air with their moans of satisfaction.

Without any more hesitation, Graveyard kicked in the door and pointed his pistol at everyone. They all jumped up with startled looks on their faces. Graveyard pointed his gun at the naked Asian woman first. *Poww!* He shot her right between the eyes. She slumped down on Vega's chest and died instantly. Before the other woman could scream, Graveyard fired his weapon and shot her in the throat. She dies with a ten-inch black dildo still stuck inside her pussy.

"Get the fuck dressed!" Graveyard told Vega. "And hurry up!"

Vega pushed Cindy's dead body to the side and started grabbing all of his clothes. He looked at the man with the hard, serious expression and didn't say a word. *If the man wanted me dead, he would've already killed me*, he thought.

Still, Vega wasn't taking any chances. After Vega got dressed, he grabbed his jacket. Inside his pocket were the three white pieces of papers, the same papers that held his most personal secrets.

"Here, put on these cuffs," Graveyard said. He watched as Vega cuffed himself in the front.

"Come on, let's go!" Graveyard said.

Vega looked over at his two dead sex freaks and shook his head. He still couldn't believe what had just happened. Then Vega looked at the man with the gun and said, "Whatever they're paying you, I'll triple it!"

"Don't say another word, you coward motherfucker!" Graveyard said, ignoring the bribe.

Vega looked into the man's eyes and saw pure evil. He had never been more scared for his life. When he walked past Graveyard, the pistol was pressed into the small of Vega's back. In front of the house, one of the black vans pulled up to the front door. When the van's door opened, Vega was immediately pushed inside, duct taped, and blindfolded like the others. Then the van pulled off down the dark, quiet street.

Two minutes later a man dressed in all black walked up to the two-story home. Inside his right hand was a hand grenade. He pulled the small pin and threw the grenade through the front window.

Booomm! The sound of the loud explosion woke the entire neighborhood. In less than a minute the house was engulfed by fire and thick, gray smoke while pieces of debris floated into the dark sky.

A block away the man got back into the waiting van. Then the driver pulled off, headed for the cemetery in North Philadelphia.

Chapter 30

10:19 PM

THE RAP SHOW AT THE Philadelphia Civic Center turned out to be a major success. There were no fights, altercations, or violence at the event, and all the rappers signed to the Underworld label had done exceptionally well, especially J-Dawg, who ripped the stage like he owned it.

After the show, most of the celebrities got back into their luxury cars and limos and headed for one of the many celebrity after parties that were taking place around the city. But Frank and Craig were not interested in going to any of the parties. They were already scheduled to attend a funeral ceremony.

The two FBI agents sat inside their unmarked car that was parked in a secluded area not far from Underworld Entertainment. Neither of them knew about all of Vega's properties being burned to the ground. They had been too busy plotting and planning their next attack, and watching the gorgeous, young black prostitutes walking back and forth across the street. When three of the prostitutes started walking toward their car, the agents looked at each other with big smiles on their faces.

"Hell, why not," Mitchell said as they both rolled down their windows.

As the three attractive, black women approached their car, Stokes began to have an erection. One of the women stood at his window while the other two stood at Mitchell's window.

"How can we help y'all ladies?" Mitchell asked as he stared at the women's large breasts.

"How about me and my two friends give you boys something to always remember us by?" one of the women asked seductively.

"Something like what?" Stokes asked as he sat there hypnotized by the woman's hour-glass figure, full lips, and sexy set of eyes.

"A message," the woman replied.

"A message from who?" Mitchell asked.

"A message from Underworld!" they said in unison. And then in one smooth motion, all three women opened their purses and pulled out their 9 mm guns with attached silencers. Then they aimed and fired every single bullet at the two FBI agents' heads and chests. Stokes's and Mitchell's bodies slumped down in their seats. Blood covered both their faces. With more than fifteen bullets inside each of them, death was instant and quiet. The three women calmly turned and walked away, disappearing into the darkness of the unforgiving city.

Frank's limousine pulled into the graveyard and headed straight to the back. When it pulled over and parked, he and Craig got out and walked over to their men, who had been waiting patiently. The three large graves were a few feet away with a large pile of dirt piled up next to each of them. Frank and Craig walked over to the middle grave and looked down at all the frightened faces inside. Each person was squirming around like a worm in the earth. They all knew that death was inevitable.

Frank and Craig walked over to the last grave. It was empty. "Go get him!" Frank commanded.

Two of his men rushed over to one of the parked vans. After snatching out Vega's body, they carried him over to Frank. Frank looked at Vega with a cold stare, feeling more hatred for Vega than he had ever felt for anyone in his entire life. Frank reached out and snatched the duct tape off of Vega's mouth.

"You coward, muthafucka!" Frank barked.

Everyone stood around watching as the two men stared at each other—hate in Frank's eyes and fear in Vega's.

"Show this stupid sonofabitch what he did to himself!" Frank said.

The two men grabbed Vega's arms and walked him over to the middle grave. When Vega looked inside, his eyes couldn't believe what they saw. Junie, Artie, Butcher, Homicide, Spade, and Canon were all handcuffed, duct taped, and grouped together like sardines in a can. Vega saw the scared looks on all their faces and painfully turned away. The two men grabbed his arms again and walked him over to the first grave. When Vega saw his pregnant wife, Raquel, and his daughter, Erika, handcuffed and duct taped as well, he fell to his knees and screamed, "Noooooooo! Nooo!"

Instantly tears started falling from his terrified eyes. He knew then that he had been fighting a winless war. Vega saw the frightened look on his wife's and daughter's faces. Tears fell from both of their scared eyes. The two men picked up Vega and carried him back over to Frank.

"Please, Frank, don't kill my family! Please!" Vega begged.

"You killed mine!" Frank said with a penetrating stare. Before Frank said another word, he was shocked to hear his named being called by a female voice.

"Underworld, come over here," the voice yelled out. "Underworld, where are you?"

Frank turned from Vega and walked over to the middle grave. Spade had somehow managed to get the duct tape off of her mouth. Frank looked down at the woman. Surprisingly, she was very attractive.

"What is it?" Frank asked.

"I just wanted to look you in the eyes and tell you I really enjoyed killing your parents," Spade said with a grin.

"And I'm really gonna enjoy watching you die tonight," Frank retorted.

"Death is life. Death has always had a prominent place in my and Canon's souls. See, for us, Underworld, dying is a very beautiful thing. You should come join us."

"No, thanks. It's not my time to go. But it is all y'all's," Frank said as he turned and walked away. Frank looked over at his men and said, "Take care of them now!"

Suddenly all of Frank's men walked over to the middle grave and surrounded it. In each of their hands were loaded 9 mm, .40 caliber, and .45 pistols. Bingo, Meatloaf, Domino, Passion, and fifteen of Frank's top men all stood over the ten-foot grave pointing their guns down below. Then the deadly fireworks began. The loud sounds of gunshots filled the dark sky like it was the Fourth of July. All six bodies inside the grave died instantly. Vega watched the scene unfold in pure terror. His hands trembled and his heart beat rapidly inside his chest.

"Fill it up," Frank told his men.

His men quickly ran over to the large piles of dirt and took out shovels. Then they started filling the large hole with the dirt. Frank turned to Vega and said, "You caused that."

"Please, Frank! Please don't kill my family!" he cried. "Please!" his voice trembled with fear.

"And why shouldn't I do that?"

"Because... because... I... I'm..."

"What, you coward, spit it out!" Frank yelled.

"Because, Frank, I'm your brother!" Vega said.

"Brother? Is that some kind of sick joke?" Frank asked, reaching out and grabbing Vega's jacket collar.

"No! It's the truth! Check the papers in my pocket and see for yourself," Vega said as tears continued to fall from his scared eyes.

Frank looked around at everyone. Confused looks covered all their faces.

"See what he's talking about, Frank. The papers are inside his pocket," Craig said.

Frank snatched the three pieces of paper out of Vega's jacket-pocket. Then Craig walked over to Frank's side, and together they started reading. One of the pieces of paper was Vega's original birth certificate. When Frank saw the signature of his parents on it, he couldn't believe his eyes. The other two pieces of paper were Vega's adoption papers, signed by a Mr. and Mrs. Littles on the day that the child became theirs, almost thirty-three years ago. Frank's parents' signatures were also on the two forms for agreeing to release the custody of their second child, Vega Cornelius Simms. Frank and Craig both stood there with bemused expressions on their faces. They were speechless.

"Where the hell did you get this?" Frank finally asked.

"A private investigator," Vega said. "Three years ago I hired a PI to find out who my birth parents were. When I found out that they were yours, I couldn't believe it. My stepbrother, Tony, was killed by your men and I was already furious with you. But after learning we had the same parents, and that we were blood brothers, it only made me hate you even more. For three long years I've been holding this personal vendetta inside, hating you and our parents more than anything in life."

"Why?" Frank asked as a lonely tear fell down the corner of his eye. "Why? Tell me why, you coward motherfucker!"

Vega looked into Frank's watery eyes and said, "Because they never loved me. They only loved you! And that's why they kept you and gave me away to complete strangers."

The words hit Frank like a ton of rocks. Brothers?

"I'm your blood, Frank, your only living relative!" Vega said.

Frank was disgusted by the revelation that Vega was his brother. "I hate you, motherfucker. Now die!" he yelled.

In a burst of rage Frank pushed Vega into the ten-foot hole. Vega fell hard, but he was still alive. Frank walked up to the hole and stared down at his heartless enemy, his younger brother. He tossed the three papers into the grave. Vega stood with the handcuffs still around his hands.

"I'm your brother, Frank. Please don't do this!" he cried out.

"You're nothing to me. Nothing!"

Everyone else stood around watching in total disbelief. No one said a word.

"Go get the snakes!" Frank said as he continued to stare down at Vega's crying face.

Three of Frank's men ran over to one of the parked vans and got inside. Then the van slowly backed up to the large hole, and the two back doors swung wide open. The two men in the back grabbed the brooms inside the truck and started sweeping the fifty large snakes down into the ten-foot hole.

"No! No! Ahh! No! Ah! Frank! No! Ah!" Vega screamed out as the snakes fell all over his body.

Vega stood there in the middle of his own manmade grave, surrounded by fifty of his biggest fears—live snakes.

"No! Ahh!" Vega shouted as he kicked off a snake that had wrapped itself around his leg. As soon as he kicked one away, two more wrapped themselves around him.

"Please, Frank! I'm your brother! Ah! Yahh!"

"Give me your gun," Frank told Graveyard. Graveyard walked over and passed him a .40 caliber. Frank looked at Vega and said, "You killed the two people I love. Now I'ma kill the two people you love!"

Then he turned and walked away.

"No, Frank, not my family! No! No!" Vega yelled out. "Please don't kill my wife and child!!"

Boom! Boom! The two loud gunshots echoed through the night.

When Vega heard the two gunshots, he fell to his knees, no longer caring about the fifty snakes that squirmed around his body. Because of his greed and hatred, his pregnant wife and child were now both dead. The decisions that he had made cost him everything and everyone he loved.

Frank walked back over to the other grave and looked down at Vega. Brother or not, he felt no remorse. All he saw was another enemy. They had been two kings playing a violent and ruthless game of chess. Now the game was finally over.

Frank passed the gun back to Graveyard and said, "Do whatchu do!" Then he and Craig turned and started walking toward the waiting limousine.

After the limousine drove off with Frank and Craig inside, Graveyard looked around at everybody still present. Then he stood at the edge of the large grave and stared down at Vega's body. Without hesitation he pointed his .40-caliber pistol at Vega's head and pulled the trigger. *Boom!* The loud explosion echoed into the darkness of the night.

Once Vega was dead, Bingo, Domino, Passion, and Meatloaf got into one of the vans and pulled off. Graveyard stood a few feet away from Vega's grave, watching the remaining men fill it with dirt.

I-95 South

"This is a small world, huh," Craig said as he passed Frank a glass of champagne.

"Very small," Frank said, taking a sip.

"Who would ever believe it, huh?"

"The world is full of many surprises, Craig. And no one knows when they'll get smacked upside the head with one."

"Well at least the war is over."

"The war is never over, Craig. There's always a new enemy lurking around the corner, watching to take an old enemy's place. We can never sleep in this game. And when we do, we must leave one eye open with a loaded gun in our hands. One thing's for sure, I own this city! And whoever tries to take it away from me will feel every bit of my wrath."

"Our wrath!" Craig said as they reached out and touched glasses.

Forty minutes later

The limousine pulled up at the front gate of the Philadelphia International Airport. Craig gave Frank a warm hug before Craig exited the car.

"Enjoy yourself out in Cali," Frank said. "And tell Janell I said hi."

"I sure will," Craig said before the door shut and he turned and walked away.

A half hour later

When Frank walked into his house, Cassie was sitting on the sofa patiently waiting for him. She had just finished watching the Fox late night news. Frank walked over and sat down beside her. They exchanged a long and passionate kiss.

"How was you day?" she asked.

"Perfect. Every day is perfect with you in it," Frank said, wrapping his arms around her shoulders. Cassie snuggled into his arms and looked deep into his eyes.

"I just got off the phone with Janell," she said. "She's waiting on Craig." She smiled.

"He'll be there in a few hours. I just dropped him off at the airport."

"Good, 'cause she can't wait," Cassie said and they both started laughing. "I just finished watching the Fox news," Cassie said, changing the subject.

"Oh, did the Phillies win?" Frank asked with a smile.

"Yeah, they beat the Mets 5-3, but that ain't what I wanted to talk about," Cassie said as she playfully pushed Frank's arm. "I saw all the houses that got blown up today. Over a dozen of them. Firemen found two dead bodies in one of them. Two women."

"Oh, really?" Frank asked, running his fingers through Cassie's long black hair.

"All the houses belong to a guy named Vega Littles. The authorities can't get in contact with him. Seems like he just up and disappeared from the face of the earth," Cassie said.

Frank leaned down and looked deep into Cassie's beautiful brown eyes. After kissing her softly on the lips, he said, "Maybe he did."

Chapter 31

Three days later

THE TINTED BLACK VAN PULLED over to the side of the road and the side doors quickly slid open. Two bodies were pushed to the cold ground. The pregnant woman and her six-year-old daughter were dressed in filthy clothes and handcuffed together at the wrists. For the last three days they rode in the van, handcuffed and blindfolded, fed only bread and water.

A passing policeman spotted the crying mother and daughter walking along the side of the road. When he noticed that they were handcuffed, he quickly pulled over his patrol car and got out.

"Are y'all okay?" the officer asked, looking into their scared faces. The officer could plainly see that they were both terrified.

"They kidnapped us!" the lady shouted. "They kidnapped us! And they killed Vega!"

The frightened young girl held on to her mother's arm, trembling uncontrollably.

"Come on. Walk over to my car," the officer said. "I have to get these handcuffs off of y'all."

They followed the officer over to his patrol car.

"Now, who kidnapped you?" he asked as he removed the cuffs with a universal key.

"I . . . don't know! They killed Vega!"

"Who's Vega?"

"My husband!" she yelled.

"OK, OK, calm down. We'll get to the bottom of this, but first I need you to tell me a few things," the officer said, taking out a pen and a small pad. "What are y'all names?" he asked.

"My name is Raquel Littles, and this is my daughter Erika Littles. I'm thirty-two and she is six."

"OK, good. Now where were y'all kidnapped?"

"From our home."

"What's the address?"

"Nineteen sixty-seven west City Line Avenue."

"Where is that?" he asked, not recognizing the address.

"Right here in Philadelphia!" Raquel answered, frustrated that the police would not know such an established Philadelphia street.

"Ma'am, I'm sorry to have to tell you this, but you're not in Philadelphia. In fact, you are nowhere near it," he said, pointing to the patrol car door.

When Raquel saw the words on the side of the patrol car, she couldn't believe her eyes. It said: THE CITY OF DETROIT POLICE DEPT.

"You're in Detroit, miss, Detroit, Michigan," the cop said.

Philadelphia, PA
Chinatown

Inside the back room of the Chinese restaurant, Bobby Chang sat at his private booth staring at the picture of his dead sister, Cindy. Everyone in the city had heard about the wipeout of Vega's entire crew. And not one of the crew members' bodies had yet to be found. Only Jewell's and Cindy's burned corpses were identified after being discovered inside the house in Southwest Philly. While the FBI was searching around for the culprits that murdered the two federal agents inside their car, Bobby Chang already knew who was responsible for Vega's sudden disappearance and his young sister dying inside the house fire—the Underworld cartel.

As Bobby sat there in tears, listening to the sound of Beethoven coming from the grand piano, Bobby thought about how he would revenge his only sister's death. And how Frank "Underworld" Simms would one day feel all of his pain.

The Federal Detention Center, Philadelphia

Two hours before the two jailhouse informants were due to go before a federal grand jury and give their sworn statements about Vega Littles's and Frank "Underworld" Simms's drug organizations, they were found inside their cells, each dead on their cots with multiple stab wounds to their mangled bodies. The entire FDC was immediately put on emergency lockdown, and an investigation of the two informants' mysterious deaths was currently underway.

On the corner of Third and Market streets, the two COs on Frank's payroll stood around waiting patiently. They were both dressed in civilian clothes—blue jeans, white T-shirts, and brown Timberland boots. Moments later a tinted black limousine pulled up to the corner and stopped. When the door opened, the COs both climbed inside. Attorney Robert Steiner and his wife Emily were inside the limo surrounded by the women of DNA. The two men didn't say a word. Robert passed them each twenty-five thousand dollars in cash, and they pocketed their money and got out of the limousine. Then they stood back and watched as the limousine slowly pulled off, headed for Atlantic City, New Jersey.

Los Angeles
The Four Seasons Hotel, Beverly Hills

Joe stood at the front door listening as the sound of intense lovemaking came form Janell's private suite. He was disgusted. Hearing Janell's pleasing moans only made him more upset and disappointed with her. For the last three days Janell had only left her suite twice, and that was to practice with her dancers for her upcoming tour. After practice she quickly climbed back into her limo and rushed back to the private suite to be with her handsome, secret lover. When Joe couldn't stand the noise anymore, he turned and walked away.

Inside the suite, Janell's and Craig's naked, sweaty bodies lay in front of the fireplace. They were both breathing hard and heavy, each shivering from the powerful orgasms that were still reverberating throughout their bodies. Janell rolled her body on top of Craig's and said, "If you keep this up, I'll never make it to my tour. And poor Joe will lose his mind."

"You're the one who wants to start up every time he comes over to the door," Craig said and smiled.

"Because I know it pisses him off." Janell grinned. "Besides, I told him about being in my personal business."

"Hey, it's fine with me," Craig said as they wrapped their arms around each other and began passionately kissing again.

Moments later Joe was standing back at the door, listening as Janell and Craig filled the air with the sounds of blissful lovemaking.

Philadelphia, PA

On the corner of Front and Girard Avenue a short, Dominican man stood there watching as people got off the SEPTA number fifteen trolley car and rushed up the stairs to catch the el train. A few feet away a blue Lincoln Navigator with two Dominican men inside was parked and waiting for Charles Lipps.

Charles Lipps was one of Philadelphia's most respected private investigators. He had a lot of legal and illegal contacts throughout the city. In fact, he was used more by drug dealers and other criminals than he was by the authorities. Charles was a forty-three-year-old tall white man, with piercing blue eyes and dark black hair. He was a cautious man who kept his eyes wide open and his ears always to the streets. Mr. Lipps calmly approached the Lincoln Navigator.

"Mr. Lipps, what did you find out?" the Dominican man asked.

"I told you, Perez, that this will all take some time. Now you and your friend will have to be more patient if you want this investigation done right."

"We don't have that much time, Mr. Lipps. Our boss gave us only a month to come up with some answers about his son's murder. Our asses are on the line here," Perez said.

"Well, Perez, right now all I have is a small hunch. But it's really nothing to get serious about," Mr. Lipps said as he looked over his shoulder to see if anyone was watching them.

"Tell me, Mr. Lipps. What's this hunch you have?" Perez asked.

"Well you heard about the Vega-Underworld war, right?"

"What war? It was a massacre!" Perez said and laughed.

"Exactly. Vega and no one in his whole crew have been found or heard from in three days, and all of his properties have been blown up and destroyed. In fact, his entire empire has been wiped off the face of the earth."

"So what does that have to do with anything?" Perez asked.

"Didn't you tell me that Vega and Carlos were friends? That Vega's connect was Carlos Benitez?" Mr. Lipps asked.

"Whoa! You don't think that Underworld put a hit out on Carlos, do you?"

"No, it's just a hunch. But who knows? I've seen a lot worse. Just think about it, Perez. What better way to destroy your enemy than by having your enemy's drug connect killed?"

"No way! We don't have no beef with the Underworld organization," Perez said.

"Y'all don't, but Vega did. And Vega was connected to Carlos."

Perez looked into Mr. Lipps's serious eyes and asked, "Do you know who Underworld is? Do you understand what you are saying?"

"Like I said, Perez, it's just a hunch. Until I find out more, right now all I have is a hunch."

The two men shook hands, and Perez got back into the Navigator and quickly sped off toward his downtown office.

Cleveland, Ohio

Sitting on his king-sized bed, Graveyard had just finished counting the twenty-five thousand dollars that Frank had paid him. It was the most money he'd ever had at any one time.

The night of the murders, after watching Frank's men fill up the graves with dirt, Graveyard left the cemetery and drove downtown. On his way to his room at the Marriott, he saw the blinking lights of police cars surrounding the shot-up car containing the two dead FBI agents. With a big smile on his face, he kept driving.

When Graveyard entered his room that night, he turned on the lights and walked over to the closet. A smile graced his face when he saw the black briefcase inside. Graveyard picked up the briefcase and sat on the bed. He opened it and saw a small piece of paper lying on top of the neat stack of fifty- and hundred-dollar bills. Graveyard picked up the paper and read it.

It said:

```
Enjoy, and thanks again for a job
well done. I'll see you when I need
you     again.   Friends   for    life.
Underworld.
```

Graveyard closed the briefcase and lay back on the bed. With his hands behind his head, he stared up at the ceiling, smiling from ear to ear.

Downtown Philly

When Cassie saw the tinted black Maybach pull up in front of the hospital, she walked out of the large glass doors and hurried over to the car. As soon as she closed the car door, Frank pulled off down the street.

"How's Valerie doing?" he asked.

"So much better. The doctor said she'll be just fine," Cassie said with a smile.

"That's good to hear," Frank said.

"So what's the big occasion?" Cassie asked, referring to Frank taking the Maybach out.

"Oh, I just wanted to get 'im out and take him for a nice long drive," Frank said.

"Long?" Cassie asked as she gave him a suspicious look.

"Yeah. A very good friend of mine said that me and a special guest can come out to his fabulous new home in the Hamptons. I figured that since it's the weekend, then why shouldn't me and my lovely fiancée get away for a few days?" Frank asked as he maneuvered the Maybach through downtown traffic.

"Oh, is that right?" Cassie asked as she got herself more comfortable in her seat.

Frank reached over and pushed the play button on the CD player. Instantly the soulful voice of Janell Jones flowed out of the car speakers. Frank looked over at Cassie's smiling face and winked. While he headed toward the New Jersey Turnpike, they both started singing the words to the song "Love Can't Wait."

"Happiness is the greatest success . . .
And success is the greatest revenge."

-Jimmy DaSaint, I.C.H.

COMING SOON

THE UNDERWORLD II: WAR OF THE BOSSES

A NOVEL BY

JIMMY DASAINT

Other Novels by Jimmy DaSaint

Black Scar Face
Black Scar Face II
Young Rich and Dangerous
On Everything I Love
Money Desire Regrets
A Rose Amongst Thorns
What Every Woman Wants

For more information go to
www.dasaintentertainment.com

In Stores Now

Get Mine or Get Naked
By Rico Salam

www.TheFirmPublication.com
215-848-4385

COMING SOON   The Sequel
"Trickin' Aint Easy" a novel by Rico Salam

To place an order for one of the books, please send a money order or cashier's check for $15.00 Ea., and $3.95 for shipping to the address below. You can also call 718-739-0284 to place an order or for wholesale orders.

COMING SOON!
Thicker Than Blood *Oct. 30*
Damaged *Nov. 15* • Tit4Tat *Dec. 1*

NEW VISION PUBLICATION
P.O. Box 310367 • Jamaica, NY 11431

www.newvisionpublication.com

For the newest selection of books at the cheapest price visit:

The Firm Publication

TheFirmPublication.com

Advertise you company with us.

BLACK SCARFACE II

Another novel by **Jimmy DaSaint**